THE

ENCLAVE

Mark Thomas

WolfSinger Publications ⸗ Brackettville, Texas

1

"It's a lovely wall, we've got no complaints there," an elderly woman said to her companion, who nodded absently.

I blinked, scrunched up my nose and wondered where I was.

For a few seconds, I watched those two women shuffling along a riverside path. They leaned towards each other, talking intently, and comingling their colourful sundresses. But when I blinked again, the women had disappeared. An invisible stage magician must have twirled his cloak because I was suddenly staring at two men preparing to fish in a brownish patch of water.

I wanted to look for the two women; I already missed them. I also wanted to examine my surroundings, but my head felt extraordinarily heavy, so I just stared at the new apparitions in front of me. The two men unfolded lawn chairs in the shade of a Maple tree, placed a tackle box and bait bucket on the ground and leaned two rods against the trunk.

One of the men was extremely old and he sat down with great care, bending limbs almost as thin as the tubes in his chair frame. The man's skin was flat and frayed like the nylon seat webbing, so when he leaned back, he looked like a second chair, stacked on top of the first.

The middle-aged man must have been his son because they had similar features. The middle-aged simulacrum baited a hook, cast the rig far into the water, then passed the rod to his father. The old man's fingers wrapped around the cork handle like curls of paper.

Then, the son cast his own line, sat down, and inclined his head towards the old man as their chairs stretched like cats waking up.

"Oh yes, it's a lovely wall," I heard a familiar voice say, somewhere to my left.

My neck was a jumble of mismatched gears, but I managed to smile and slowly turn towards the sound. The two women, the ones I had seen when I first opened my eyes, were still plodding along that stone pathway. They hadn't vanished, just moved outside my constricted field of vision. Both women favored their right legs, as if convalescing from identical injuries. They carried folding chairs, hooked over their arms like purses, and pointed at various trees, choosing a spot to sit and stare at the water, themselves.

"We've no complaints, there. It's a lovely wall." They paused underneath an enormous Willow, snicked their chairs open, sat down and sighed. "No complaints at all." Then, yellow and green-budded tendrils obscured them, like a beaded privacy screen. I took a deep breath and rotated my head back to the fishermen.

"Thank you," the older man said. He had a surprisingly firm voice. He slowly extended one cluster of paper fingers over the tackle box and bait bucket, to squeeze the younger man's wrist. They seemed utterly content in this little parkette, with their lines in the brown water, one taking care of the other, and their chairs making small animal noises.

The scenery in front of me was both familiar and strange like a landscape in a dream. The river was broad but probably shallow because black branches protruded from the surface quite a distance from shore. Erosion must have snatched some trees from the bank and anchored their corpses in the mud. In fact, the nearby Maple was leaning towards the water like a swimmer trying to work up the nerve to dive in and join his friends.

I looked down, mildly surprised to discover *I* was sitting in a lawn chair, as well. I must have fallen asleep in the sun and was now struggling to crawl back to consciousness. A book was open on my lap: *Remarkable History of the Sextant* by Admiral George Fielding Elliot. I seemed to be halfway through the volume but couldn't remember anything I'd read.

I tilted my chin up a few degrees, and my skull moved in small, discrete increments.

The opposite riverbank was lined with golden bullrushes. Blackbirds with bright red shoulder patches flitted amongst the stalks, and ducks poked at floating pondweed. Beyond the tangle of shore plants there was a sloping farm field covered with a thick, low-growing crop, perhaps soybeans.

A dozen enormous wind turbines stood in that field like robot space invaders, patiently awaiting orders. Their blades turned very slowly, finding wind currents a hundred feet above the ground. There was a line of spindly trees at the back of the field and beyond that, purpled by distance, was the wall.

I might not have noticed the structure at all, if those women hadn't mentioned it several times. The wall was remarkable, but it was also strangely unobtrusive, like a bank of clouds or an escarpment ridge.

In the direction I was looking, the wall was at least a mile away. It was quite tall, perhaps seventy or eighty feet, and had a scalloped top, a series of large semi-circles that looked like cake decoration. The wall gently curled beyond my peripheral vision.

I raised my right arm and stared at the hand hanging from the end of it. The appendage seemed almost as strange and remote as the wall. I moved the hand towards my face like a crane operator manipulates a boom, and used stiff fingers to massage the muscles under my jaw. Whisker stubble made a soft, scratchy noise.

I forced my head left again, like a damaged tank turret, and looked past the Willow tree where those two elderly women were sitting. I saw a small, paved parking platform and a row of waterfront cottages. The wall traversed the river, there, like a gigantic dam, and brown water flowed into a dozen semicircular depressions, that might have been intake portals for a hydro-electric generator. Those openings had canted metal grills to deflect debris, and an orange buoy-line that warned off careless boaters or swimmers.

But there were no boaters or swimmers.

This section of the wall was close enough for me to see a distinct pattern of horizontal and vertical lines. The colour was variegated, brown, grey and green, with lighter splotches near the top where it was weathered.

It was impossible to make sense of the wall, so my brain occupied itself with trivial observations and inferences instead. The wall obviously predated its spindly-tree border, but it wasn't centuries old, like a medieval castle. In fact, the structure looked modern and utilitarian, an assemblage of interlocking panels nested within metal rails. It was the kind of thing that might be used, on a much smaller scale, as a sound barrier near a highway.

The wall was thin, at least the edges of the semi-circular scallops gave that impression. Of course, it might have been bulkier near the base.

I rotated my shoulders, shifted position in the lawn chair, and turned back to the fishermen. The old man's colourful float was now darting about the surface of the water. When his son nudged him, the old man cranked his reel handle. The younger man got out of his chair and stepped down to the riverbank to help land the fish. He grabbed the line and pulled a wriggling perch into the air. The fish had a brilliant yellow belly and glistening black side bars. Both men smiled, the fish was unhooked, and tossed onto the grass near the trunk of their shade tree. The perch flopped several times as the younger man re-baited the old guy's hook and re-cast.

"How's the fishing?" A stout lady materialized, from the right. She stood with her hands on her hips and squinted at the men.

"Not so bad," the old man said. He waved at the fish twitching near the base of the Maple, and I noticed there were several other fat perch in the grass.

I wondered if I had been periodically falling asleep and missing bits of the action.

"You're going to have a nice fish fry tonight," the woman said then waddled along the path towards the spot where the river flowed through the wall.

"Yes, yes, yes." I could only see the back of the old man's head, but I could tell he was smiling. "There's nothing better than fresh, pan-fried perch." The man's words instantly evoked a memory of crispy pectoral fins that snapped like potato chips when bitten.

I had no idea where that memory came from. I had no idea where I was, or why I was sitting in a small park staring at a patch of brown water. I didn't know *who* I was either, but that deficiency didn't make itself known until later. The strangest thing about my situation was the sense of calm in the face of so much potential angst. The mention of a fish fry made me feel slightly hungry, but even that physical need wasn't pressing.

I glanced down at the book lying in my lap, but I could no longer read the title because all of the letters had somehow wriggled into unfamiliar positions.

Maybe I'd suffered a stroke, or some other brain injury that impacted my language centres.

But I didn't feel particularly ill, just a little stiff. Perhaps the letter-scrambling was nothing more than a response to eye strain.

I immediately checked the top of my head for a pair of reading glasses. Nothing but hair. I checked the folds of clothing underneath the book, then let my fingers trail through the nearby patches of grass, but they only encountered an empty take-out coffee container.

Gingerly, I stood up. My legs felt strong. I did a deep knee bend, then repeated the action, one leg at a time, lowering my body about a foot. I opened and closed each hand and each eye individually. There wasn't any one-side paralysis, no tell-tale muscle twitching.

But it was disconcerting to have a book title turn into a handful of writhing bait worms. I rubbed the stubble on my chin again. I hadn't shaved today, perhaps not for several days.

I sat down again, and my chair creaked in a friendly way.

The fishermen's bait bucket had the phrase "TWO DOZEN" written on it in red, blocky letters. I was able to read *that*; perhaps the colour or distance was helpful. Or maybe my bout of alexia was just a momentary spasm. I decided to take another stab at the *Remarkable History of the Sextant* but, strangely, couldn't locate it.

Admiral George Fielding Elliot had vanished.

I'd *just* put the book down when I stood up to do my knee bends; it should be floating somewhere nearby, not missing in action like a ship piloted without a sextant.

This wasn't the muzziness one might expect after waking up from a nap in the sun, this was more like a real medical crisis. Bits of the world, both significant and trivial, were playing hide and seek.

I imagined a nurse gently questioning me as if I were a badly injured patient, newly-arrived on the ward: "Do you know where you are, right now, dear? …Oh, no, you're in a hospital…Do you know what city the hospital is in? No…that's the wrong country. Do you know why you're here? …No, that's hardly likely, is it?"

There was obviously something wrong with me but at least the impairment had limits. For example, I knew what a hospital was, and I knew hospitals had employees called nurses who asked condescending triage questions. I knew the creature flopping on the parkette grass was a fish, and an unusually large specimen of a specific species. When I looked at the wall, I knew it was a wall, not a cliff, or part of a building, and I could speculate about its age and how it was constructed.

The wall's purpose eluded me, but at least I was aware that things tended to have purpose, I wasn't quite as badly off as the perch gasping and dying in this alien environment.

I scratched the beard stubble.

Yes, walls have purpose. I listed a few possibilities: walls keep some things out and other things in; for example, they reduce highway noise near over-priced subdivisions; they also delineate property; they defend borders; they warehouse zoo animals and criminals.

But generally, walls weren't as tall as the one looming to my left.

Then, an odd image popped into my consciousness. I found myself thinking about the perimeter wall of the Dachau concentration camp, and how it wasn't high and imposing, like you might expect. In fact, it was rather stubby, as if daring prisoners to scramble over the top. That temptation was perverse, however, because broken glass was imbedded in the cement coping, and spirals of razor wire waited on the other side. I could visualize that wire, now, corpse-speckled like a giant spool of flypaper.

Interesting.

My brain obviously had random bits of information shoved underneath the basement stairs, just waiting to be pulled into the open. A glimpse of the strange wall in this parkette had somehow dredged up mental pictures of those old Nazi fortifications. It was an odd association of ideas because the physical structures were very different, and they had very different auras. This parkette was a suburban Eden, while Dachau was a miserable death camp.

I scratched at my neck stubble. Maybe I was in a sanctuary and the wall was protecting me from nasty creatures on the other side, beings who were slathering to get inside and feast.

An elderly man, twenty or thirty meters to my right, yawned noisily and folded a blanket. He didn't seem particularly worried about invaders.

"You've found a beautiful spot to sit and read," a woman said. I twisted in my chair and saw the visitor's smiling face. She held my lost book in her pudgy fingers and extended her arm towards me. Letters on the cover were behaving themselves once again, *George Eliot,* was visible and stable.

"Thank you, very much," I said, reaching for the volume. I

petted it, and placed it on the grass between my feet, so it wouldn't wander off again.

"You're welcome." The lady rocked gently from side to side.

Her response meant I'd produced intelligible noises, which was a relief. I had already rejected the "stroke" hypothesis, but it's comforting to have your theories confirmed. "I'm eager to finish the book, but I seem to have lost my glasses."

"I wish you good luck, but I won't help look," the woman said. "My own eyesight is poor and I'm likely to tread on them." She pivoted forward, treating me to a polite, aristocratic bow. "Good day." She talked with the indeterminate accent of old movies where characters are supposed to be European but have to speak English for the convenience of the audience.

I tried to recall a clumsy foreign character in a movie to make a more detailed comparison but couldn't. In fact, I couldn't recall *any* film title, plot, character, trailer or poster. I knew what all of those things were, but the mental files fleshing out such generalities were completely empty.

Astounding.

"Come along Kazimir."

A little bulldog hobbled towards the woman, trailing a leash. The animal had wandered underneath the younger fisherman's chair to sniff perch slime. The bulldog looked up at me with wet eyes, and the corners of his mouth lifted in a subtle dog-smile that seemed to be asking me where *my* leash was.

"Good day." The pair lumbered out of my visual field. The woman walked with a pronounced limp, and the little dog had a hobble-step that was a comic imitation of her gait. They disappeared behind the willow tree.

I shook my head.

This mental disseverment was extraordinary. How was it possible to know what a "movie" was, without being able to remember a single, specific example? How could I mentally reconstruct a WWII concentration camp without being able to recall which countries were involved in that conflict?

Similarly, I knew fathers and sons sometimes went fishing together, but I didn't know if I had a father or son, myself. I couldn't even feel sad imagining a loss.

I continued my half-hearted search for the potentially missing glasses. I stuck my hand into a pocket, felt a bulge, and pulled out a wad of bills. I unfolded more than two hundred dollars in newish American currency. Harriet Tubman's face was on the twenty-dollar bill, and she looked disoriented, as if she had just woken from a nap and found herself inside a large walled compound. I wished she was here beside me, not just in my pockets, so we could discuss the situation.

The old man in front of me hooked another perch and his companion stepped down to the bank to unhook it. They finally had enough for their supper because the younger man began packing up their tackle.

Then, the red bait-bucket letters squirmed all over the container surface, much as the letters on my book cover had done, earlier. I rubbed my eyes; I really needed to test-drive a pair of glasses.

"See better, understand better," a voice inside my skull whispered.

I stood up, turned around, and saw a row of shops across the road from the park. One of the stores was a small pharmacy. The letters on that distant sign were large, quiet, and easy to read: PharmaSave.

I quickly looked back at the bait bucket. It was tucked under the younger man's arm, but I distinctly saw the word "wooden." The two men walked towards the row of little cottages. The son juggled all of their equipment and still managed to place a hand on his father's elbow to prevent him sliding into the river.

Back to the pharmacy. Mental associations started snicking into place, like slides in an old-fashioned carousel projector. I was suddenly positive pharmacies sold reading glasses. They typically had a display somewhere in the front of the store, near the cash register.

I surveyed the row of shops, while walking through the parkette. There was a small clothing boutique, with racks of blouses displayed on the sidewalk; there was a store that sold board games and playing cards; there was a bakery with trays of croissants angled in the front window; a laundromat, and, of course, the pharmacy.

I paused on the sidewalk for an instant to check both ways for oncoming vehicles.

That instinctive action made me smile. Caution was a habit developed over time, so I must have once lived in a large city with hazardous traffic.

But here, there wasn't a single car.

The road was broad, freshly paved and marked with a center line, but there were absolutely no vehicles. No delivery vans, no cars, no buses, no appliance repair trucks, no scooters…there wasn't even ambient noise from distant machinery.

I smiled again, but I'm not sure why the deserted street struck me as funny.

Perhaps, at some level, my brain accepted the artificiality of this neighbourhood as one might appreciate an elaborate practical joke. Of course, I didn't have any detailed memories of a more "authentic" neighbourhood to use for comparison, all I had were scraps of generalized knowledge.

At any rate, this walled community seemed like a stage set rather than an actual town, but my brain wasn't inordinately troubled, it seemed willing to relax and enjoy the show. I walked across the empty road and entered the pharmacy. There was a single cash register in front of four aisles of household products. I peeked down one row and saw a dispensary along the back wall. A man wearing mini binoculars stood like a monolith behind a high counter and stared at a beaker of swirling liquid.

He must be the pharmacist.

Sure enough, the reading glasses were in a revolving hexagonal display, at the head of a panty-hose aisle. Sunlight glinted off several mirrors, where customers could evaluate their new frames.

"Can I help you?" A young woman wearing an employee's smock and blurry name tag appeared from a make-up aisle and smiled at me. She was roughly thirty years old, by far the youngest person I had encountered in my ersatz town.

That was an odd realization.

There were no children playing in the parkette, all the people I saw were elderly or middle-aged. My own reflection in the eyeglass-stand mirror suggested I was about forty, and I was definitely skewing the average age lower. Maybe I had infiltrated a retirement community.

I smiled at the woman. "I just woke up from a nap and had difficulty reading my book. I must have misplaced my glasses."

The young woman smiled back. "What were you reading?" Her voice was all innocent curiosity.

"It's…" I wanted to show her the book but, of course, my fist was empty. I had somehow lost the book, again, in the parkette grass. I also realized I had left the chair and coffee cup behind, which was inconsiderate. And, now, I couldn't even remember the book's title. "I guess it's still in that little park across the street," I said. I turned away to hide my embarrassment and chose a pair of glasses at random, then tested the magnification on some writing samples near the top of the display.

Perfect.

"They look good," the woman said. "Would you like something else to read? Maybe a newspaper?"

For some reason, her suggestion surprised me. "Yes, I'd appreciate it. I've been sort of confused since I woke up. In fact, I don't know where I am."

Maybe I didn't project my distress very well, because the woman wasn't at all shocked, she merely smiled some more. "Well, maybe this will help." She held up a slender paper with the banner "Ttupak Enclave." It looked amateurish, like something mimeographed in a basement.

I saw a copy of The New York Times in a wooden display rack, behind her. "I'd rather have that," I said, pointing.

"Sure." She grabbed a copy and handed it to me. "The war news looks good."

War? The word shocked me. "Thanks." The newspaper was an "International Edition" with the banner date: May 21, 2037. That didn't feel right, but I couldn't refine the misgiving. Did my brain consider the date ancient history or a future projection? I didn't know, it just wasn't *right*. I walked to the cash register and saw racks of familiar impulse-buys: chocolate bars, candies, breath mints and gum. If there was a war, it hadn't resulted in WWII-style sugar shortages.

The cashier took my new glasses so she could scan the tag but that meant I couldn't read the tiny price figures on her register's display screen. I handed her two Harriet Tubmans.

"Oh," the young woman said, "did you lose your card?"

"I'm not sure." I had no idea what card she was talking about. "I just checked my pockets, and all I had was some cash."

"We're not really using cash anymore," she said. "We just swipe your card."

"Hmmm." We seemed to be at an impasse, but neither of us was particularly upset.

"Did you check the lost and found window?"

"No."

"Well, let's have a look." The young woman led me outside, onto the sidewalk. She pointed to a sign posted in the pharmacy window, just to the right of the entrance doors. The label was large enough for me to read with naked eyeballs: **Lost ID Cards**. Half a dozen plastic rectangles were affixed to the sign. One, in the bottom right-hand corner, had my face, or I should say, the face I had recently seen in a glasses-display mirror.

"There you are," the young woman said, pointing with a bright pink nail.

We re-entered the store, she flipped the sign around and pulled my card free. The young woman wiped a spot of adhesive from the plastic with her sleeve as she walked to the register. She scanned the card and handed over my purchases.

I put the glasses on. "Thank you, Kelly." I could now read her name tag. Next, I examined my ID card. The name underneath the expressionless mug shot said "Allan Ripke." Mr. Ripke was one hundred and eighty-five centimeters tall, had grey eyes, and was forty-one years old. There was an address, nine Walnut Street-unit three, but no city or state. I assumed I was in the United States because of the money stuffed into my pocket, but that wasn't a guarantee of location. Another mental slide clicked into place: lots of countries accepted, even preferred American currency.

"I've seen you in here before, but I don't think we've ever talked. It's nice to meet you, Allan." Kelly stuck out a small pale hand and we shook, very deliberately, pumping hard twice then letting go.

Kelly wasn't in a hurry to get back to work. "It's a lovely day," she said.

I screwed up my courage. "Do you ever find it weird," I asked her, "to live underneath a giant wall?"

"Well…it's a lovely wall, you have to admit. In the evening, the colour variations are really quite beautiful."

"Yes, of course." I didn't know how to respond. But, in a way, Kelly had answered my question. She didn't consider the wall to be strange, or scary, it was just *there*, a familiar part of the landscape. "I guess I'll go back to the park and get my book." I touched the new glasses. "I'll be able to finish reading, now." I looked back at the dispensary area. I could now see the pharmacist's name written in light blue letters on a darker blue bulkhead: Dr. Crecy. The pharmacist didn't include a first initial in his name, he was all business.

"Goodbye," Kelly said. "I'll probably see you tomorrow."

"Sure." I would definitely come back to the pharmacy, just to see a familiar, friendly face. So far, in this fragment of my existence, Kelly was the only person I knew. Still, I didn't know her well enough to grab her shoulders and demand an explanation for my sudden appearance in an "Enclave" surrounded by a high, but lovely, wall.

I wasn't self-conscious about having amnesia, if that's what it was. The slide carousel of ancient knowledge clicked and rotated within my skull-theatre. There was nothing shameful about suffering a mental health crisis, I was suddenly very sure of that. But little tendrils of paranoia stopped me from asking for help.

I remembered an old children's fairy tale called the "Emperor's New Clothes." It was about some self-important medieval despot who wandered around his kingdom completely naked, his dick and balls slapping against his thighs, all because no one had the guts to point out he had been conned by a tailor.

People here were a lot like those fairy-tale villagers, suspiciously compliant.

People shouldn't have been casually mentioning what a nice wall they had, they should have been saying something like: "why the fuck are we surrounded by a wall in the first place?" Whatever was happening to me, the villagers were potentially complicit, they couldn't be trusted.

But the more I thought about it, the parallel wasn't exact. The people in my community weren't *scared* to mention the wall, they just didn't seem to think it was important.

Once again, I looked both ways before jogging across the empty road. I had only been gone from the parkette for fifteen or twenty minutes, but my lawn chair had vanished. The coffee cup was still gently rolling in the grass, so I hadn't mistaken the location. I took a few steps towards the river and saw a cloud of flies buzzing over the fish slime, where the father and son angling team had deposited their catch.

I was definitely in the right place.

Perhaps I had co-opted someone else's chair, book and coffee, then fallen into a deep sleep. And maybe that person had been politely waiting for me to leave in order to retrieve his, or her, possessions. That scenario explained one minor mystery, why I couldn't recall anything from a book I was supposedly in the middle of reading.

I picked up the coffee cup and was pleased to see it was compostable, not planet-killing waxy cardboard.

The people in this community cared about the environment; that was encouraging.

I saw a garbage can, next to the small parking platform. As I walked closer, I could read a message encircling the opening: "We Recycle Everything!!!" I dropped the coffee cup in, but also leaned over, to see what type of refuse my new community produced. The receptacle held a collection of paper wrappings that must have come from the bakery, and a pair of sandals with a broken toe-strap.

I think I half expected to see my book and lawn chair jammed into the metal drum.

The parking platform was a puzzle, in itself. There were fresh yellow lines on the pavement delineating a dozen spots, but no vehicles.

I walked along the river, passing several people in lawn chairs. They were doing crossword puzzles, reading books, knitting or chatting quietly. They were all elderly, or heading in that direction, and they all looked happy.

I sat down on the riverbank, near the point where the wall crossed the water. Here, the structure was as tall as a skyscraper, I looked up but could barely see the scalloped crest. The wall veered right on the near bank, then angled left and mostly disappeared behind scattered trees and a church steeple. The degree of curvature led me to believe the enclosure was a sloppy circle, and its diameter wasn't expansive. In a way, it would have been interesting to hike around the circumference but, for some reason, I didn't have any desire to do that.

I looked at the newspaper. The front page had several articles about the "war" Kelly had mentioned. There were troop movements on the Andaman Islands and, apparently, Nigeria was using the archipelago to stage an invasion on the Indian subcontinent. But it didn't sound like a mass-landing of infantry because "Kestrels" and "Goshawks" were mentioned several times and they seemed to be military drones rather than troop transports.

It was impossible to tell from the tone of the article if *The New York Times* considered one of the combatants an ally and the other an enemy. Maybe the U.S. was remaining neutral in the conflict.

Apparently, there was a lull in the fighting in both the Somalian and Nepalese theaters but Madras was going to bear the brunt of this new offensive. Peace negotiations were supposedly on-going even as Kestrels and Goshawks flocked at their embarkation points.

The information was strangely difficult to process. It seemed utterly ridiculous to me that Nigeria and India would be at war. The two countries didn't share a border; they didn't even share a continent. I was vaguely aware both were populous and large, as well as being ascending powers on the globe. But I also had a strong feeling they were multi-ethnic and multi-religious conglomerations. It didn't seem likely either would be able to stir up enough monolithic hatred to initiate a war. One of the articles mentioned this was the fourth full year of the conflict and we were approaching the anniversary of the "Delta" incident, whatever that was. I knew the Niger River had a complex mouth. Maybe that was the site of an initial skirmish that had escalated.

The only other issue that merited front-page space was a shortage of agricultural workers that had reached a "critical" stage. The Surgeon General (Surgeon General?) made oblique references to "unconventional" solutions, but didn't provide any specific plans.

Typical politician.

I gave up and turned to the entertainment pages.

There were several colourful ads for Broadway musical productions, and I found that comforting, even though the titles were unfamiliar: "The Lodger", "Inter-Meme", "Martian Slutfest—the Musical."

I tried to read a book review for something called "The Eight-Kitten Christmas." The reviewer really liked it and provided a brief plot synopsis. Apparently, the book starts out with the main character crushing his pet kitten in a bizarre pull-out sofa-bed accident. Then, backing his car out of the driveway to take the injured animal to the veterinarian, he runs over his neighbor's tabby. The guy panics, spins his wheels and actually sprays fur and viscera all over the cat-owner's front porch. The reviewer didn't mention that it was a dark comedy or a satire, "The Eight-Kitten Christmas" seemed to be a straight-forward story about the evisceration of eight kittens leading up to Christmas.

I stopped reading.

Maybe the magnification of my new glasses wasn't as good as I'd thought at first, because I had a slight headache.

I checked carefully for traffic and re-crossed the deserted street. There was a more sophisticated recycling bin just to the right of the bakery door. As I inserted the newspaper into the slot a mechanism gently pulled it from my fingers. Then there was a soft buzz and a waft of ozone, as if the newspaper had been atomized.

I wasn't hungry, thirsty or cold but I thought it would be delightful to get a coffee and piece of pastry from the bakery. Something buried deep within my psyche wanted comfort food.

A little bell tinkled when I pushed the door open.

"Hey, Rip." A man behind the counter knew me well enough to use a nickname. "Someone found your card in the park. I told them to take it to the PharmaSave."

I got close enough to read the man's name tag. "Thanks, Kyle," I said.

"I've got some more blueberry turnovers, just out of the oven. Would you like another coffee?"

I nodded. I really should have flopped on the floor and shouted that my name wasn't Allan Ripke, it was Rip van Winkle. I should have begged this friendly person for help.

But low-grade paranoia was crawling around my skull and emitting little warning noises. "Can you really trust Kyle?" my skull-creature asked. "For all you know, he's a willing participant in this construction, this contrivance."

But there was also a strange lethargy tangled up with the burgeoning psychosis. "It *is* a nice-looking wall," a lazy voice inside my head whispered.

"Give me the usual," I said.

The proprietor steamed some beans and poured a shot of espresso into a cup with hot water and oat milk. I wondered if my alter ego, Allan Ripke, preferred oat milk to conventional dairy products or if there really was some sort of narrow wartime shortage.

"The War news is good," Kyle said, as if he were reading my mind.

I wanted to ask Kyle if we were rooting for Nigeria or India, or neither, in the conflict, but decided circumspection was the wiser course. Surely, I could figure out who the bad guy was by paying attention to scraps of conversation.

The coffee was placed on the counter along with a bumpy jam-filled pastry. I gave Kyle my card and he scanned it, then gave me a big smile. He didn't mention how much the pastry cost and didn't offer a receipt. Those latent expectations must have been two more memory scraps from my previous world, like the internal reference to Rip van Winkle.

"Thank you." The shop door was difficult to manage because my hands were full of coffee, pastry, and glasses, and there wasn't an automatic opener. But I made it and went back to the parkette. I no longer had a lawn chair so I leaned against the trunk of a tree, which was pleasant enough. I made sure to choose one that didn't have fish slime underneath it.

The wind turbines in the soy field were spinning faster now, in an escalating breeze and there was an interesting mixture of odours blowing across the water. Of course, water has its own special smell, as do bullrushes and soybeans. But my nose detected a hint of something metallic as well. It made me wonder if there was an industrial complex on the other side of the wall. There were no smoke plumes, however, and no penetrating mechanical thrum from invisible machinery, so maybe I was imagining it.

The coffee and pastry were wonderful.

I got such a pleasurable endorphin rush I wondered if the food was laced with some sort of psychotic medication. But I talked myself down from that particular clock tower. If the food was drugged, there wasn't much I could do about it now, the chemicals had already entered my bloodstream.

I watched a squirrel leap from one high branch to another in a nearby tree. The creature actually misjudged his landing and almost plummeted to the ground, but he managed to grab some spindly twigs on the way down and swing back to safety.

That near-accident made me think. If I was really worried about drugged food, I could always trap squirrels or catch some perch and butcher my meals. But that seemed like an awful lot of work. Perhaps, I could just self-monitor and see if my perceptions changed when I got hungry.

When I finished the coffee and pastry, I walked back to the parking-area garbage can to get rid of the packaging. I glanced inside the barrel again and saw it was empty. In the last half hour someone had removed the handful of wrappers and broken sandal.

A man in bright orange coveralls was sweeping dust motes from the curb of the unused street. He had a pushcart with a large trash hopper mounted on the front. We made eye-contact, and he waved with his broom hand. He also tried to generate a smile, but his expression just reminded me of the gasping Perch.

The address etched on the back of my ID card was nine Walnut Street, unit three. I might as well have a look through Allan Ripke's life, maybe his furniture and possessions would trigger some useful memories. Balsam Street bordered the Parkette, and Alder Street ran perpendicular, right beside the PharmaSave. I walked a few short blocks down Alder, glancing right and left as I passed Catalpa, Dogwood, and Elm Street. There were a dozen houses on each, as well as bumpy vacant lots that looked like old foundations in-filled with rubble. There was a lot of open meadow-area, full of purple violets and pink clover. "Heart's Ease" a voice in my brain said, "the pink clover is called Heartsease." I passed Linden, Maple, and Pine Streets. I was starting to sense an alpha-betic tree-trend and, sure enough, Walnut was between Viburnum and Yew.

As I turned down Walnut Street, I heard the clicking of foot-steps. I looked over my shoulder and saw the pharmacist, Doctor Crecy, plodding down Alder Street. Of course, he was no longer wearing the mini binoculars, but he still wore his lab coat and he moved stiffly, as I somehow knew he would. The man was carry-ing a small white paper bag in his right hand, as if he was making a delivery to a shut-in. Dr. Crecy momentarily glanced at me, inclined his head and clicked past.

Nine Walnut was a brick two-story with a wrap-around porch.

It must have been an impressive single-family home once, but now it was subdivided into five apartments, judging by the mailboxes mounted next to the main entrance door. I stuck my hand into the box numbered three, but it was empty.

My unit was at the top of a rear exterior stairway. I didn't have an entry key, but that didn't matter because there was no visible keyhole. Rather, a card reader was mounted on the doorframe. I inserted my card and the door popped open with a delicate hiss of air.

I felt a small surge of guilt while stepping across the threshold, because one of my personality fragments was spying on another. My unit was really just a large room. There was a bed, one padded chair, a small table with another unpadded chair and a tiny closet. The closet held a few shirts, pairs of pants and sweaters all neatly hung. Socks and underwear were in fabric-lined boxes.

There was no arctic-weather clothing like parkas and boots. I pulled on one of the sweaters, figuring it might get chilly, later this evening.

There was a very small bathroom with a sink, toilet and shower. The shower was a glass tube, barely large enough to hold a soapy body.

Alan Ripke didn't possess a towel, toilet paper, soap, toothbrush, moisturizer, ointment or medicine. In fact, my alter-ego seemed to have decamped.

I wondered where I had moved.

I could have knocked on the door of apartment number two and asked, I suppose, but a suspicious fold of my cortex warned me not to. I sat at my(?) table, which was positioned in front of the only window, and stared at the slightly warped Formica surface. There were heat scars and wear marks and stains that collectively formed a beautiful abstract pattern, like a newly formed galaxy whirling in table space.

Then I fell asleep. There was no intermediate period of drowsiness, I simply lost consciousness.

When I woke, I could sense it had been a long nap. The air *felt* different, and black shadows from a neighboring tree had crawled through the window and were reaching across the table, almost touching my hand. I quickly withdrew my fingers, stood up and experienced a sudden, powerful urge to leave this apartment, this Cuckoo's nest. I pushed the door open and stepped onto the landing. The door closed behind me with a soft hiss. I rattled down the staircase and stood in the small, fenced rear yard. I felt hairs rise on my neck and arms, which was an odd physiological response to something as ordinary as twilight.

I walked back to Alder Street and headed towards the river. But the needle-like steeple of a church tugged at my attention. In a way, that was natural, because it was the tallest element in the nearby landscape, but the attraction wasn't as spontaneous or random as I thought.

Without fully understanding why, I turned down Larch Street, and walked towards the church.

A number of people on this block were outside tending gardens or filling birdfeeders, but they all stopped working as I walked past. No one stared at me, however, they all simply paused, then slowly walked up the steps to their front doors. Everyone seemed to simultaneously decide it was time to roost.

That was certainly strange.

I happened to look up at the sky and saw it was thick with birds. In fact, it probably wasn't quite as late as I thought, because the sky was artificially darkened by thousands of birds that had taken wing. Sparrows, Grackles, Finches and Blackbirds flew quick, violent patterns over the roof tops. Ducks, Geese, Herons and gulls circled in a second avian layer. Higher still, Vultures, Goshawks, Osprey and Eagles corkscrewed towards the clouds, descended, then rose again.

At first, I thought it was some sort of weird feeding frenzy because clouds of insects had also risen into the air. But the birds didn't seem to be actively feeding on the bugs, or each other, they just flew about, each group producing their own distinct patterns.

Then the squirrels started climbing.

I heard their claws snicking as they scrambled up poles, climbed roofs, then leapt from roofs to trees. The animals collected near the topmost branches and chattered at each other.

It seemed to me the animal world was responding to an invisible danger signal: they knew a storm was coming and safety lay in elevation. That was counterintuitive, you'd think the safest place to be in bad weather would be close to the ground. But then I considered the high perimeter wall. Was it intended to shield us from a Biblical Tsunami?

You shouldn't own paranoia if you're unwilling to let it run around the yard.

I quickly moved to the church, feeling an impulse to climb to the very top of the steeple, like a nervous raccoon.

Unfortunately, the front door of the church was locked, and wrapped with orange caution tape. A notice fixed to the door said: "Danger. Saint Jude's Cathedral is under renovation. Do not enter under any circumstances." There was some construction litter at the side of the doorway, a small pile of bricks, and some boards stained with concrete residue. But there didn't seem to be any actual job-site activity. There was no scaffolding, fencing, machinery or tools.

A piece of cloudy plastic flapped in a window opening a dozen feet above my head. Maybe I could climb through that window and circumvent the door altogether.

But I needed a ladder.

There was no logical reason for me to peek over the fence into a neighboring yard, I can only assume I been foraging there earlier, before my river-nap, and memories of that activity were hiding but not utterly lost.

Indeed, there was a rickety wooden ladder hanging from hooks on the neighbor's side of the fence. I reached over and pulled the contraption into the church yard. I leaned the ladder against the tower; it just barely reached the window ledge with the flapping plastic. I was a little scared climbing up the ladder. Partly I was worried the fragile rungs wouldn't be able to hold my weight, but it was also apparent Allan Ripke had a fear of heights. I rolled through the ripped piece of plastic onto a strip of plank flooring about a meter wide. I had expected to see a cramped set of winding stairs, but there was nothing more than that flange and a lot of empty space. If I had rolled any further, I would have fallen to the main floor and shattered myself on the flagstones, unless a flock of angels decided to catch me.

There were black marks on the interior bricks, ghosts of an old support system, but the staircase itself had been removed.

Looking upwards, I could see a higher section of stairs was still intact, it was only the lower flights that had been dismantled.

I pulled my flimsy wooden ladder upwards, through the window. When wooden feet were firmly positioned on wooden flange, and the top rails were wedged against the brick on the opposite wall, it was possible to reach that upper staircase. I crawled up the incline, experiencing violent twinges of vertigo as my brain registered the two blocks of emptiness beneath me. I had to intently focus on each hand and toe transfer.

At the top of the ladder, I was able to squeeze my body between the exterior wall and the iron rails of a spiral staircase. I bounced one foot lightly on the bottom step to make sure the structure wouldn't collapse, then climbed up to the tower belfry. A trap door at the stair top was open and I pulled myself through, and wound up directly underneath an enormous, heavily oxidized metal bell. I closed the trap door, stood on my toes, and was able to touch the clapper, which was fused to the bell's metal lip.

The tower had four openings, screened with broken bits of wooden lattice.

I looked around. As I suspected, the (lovely) wall encircled a small network of streets, with a few hundred houses, a handful of commercial buildings and a lot of open fields. It wasn't a perfect circle, rather a choppy oval with my church positioned roughly in the center. The widest distance across might have been three miles.

I was now at least fifty feet in the air, but that wasn't high enough to see what was on the other side of the wall. Anyway, my enclave must have been in a geographical low spot, because a lazy river flowed through it. It was foolish to think I would be able to see much, even from this perch. It was possible to infer, however, that the surrounding land was pretty flat, perhaps an expansive prairie or desert.

The setting sun bounced off a reflective object just outside the western wall, and the flash momentarily blinded me.

Was I living on the margin of an enormous ice sheet or salt plain? Impossible, the weather was too moderate. I could have peeled off my sweater and been perfectly comfortable.

I sat down on a box bench and wondered what I should do next. I shifted position slightly, and the wooden seat shifted with me. I realized I was sitting on the lid of a storage container. I got up, lifted the lid and saw a sleeping bag, foam pad and a plastic bucket containing soap, ointment, toothbrush and a large bottle of water.

I unscrewed the top of the water jug and sniffed. It seemed fresh.

Several twenty-dollar bills were stuck to the bottom of the jug. I looked into the storage bench and saw more bills stuffed into crevices.

Someone was squatting at the top of this church tower; someone who didn't realize he was living in a cashless society.

Unless another head poked through the trap door opening in the next few minutes, I was willing to assume the tenant was Allan Ripke...me.

Suddenly, there was a bright moon; I must have fallen asleep again.

My brain scrolled through more bits of stored information. I was obviously narcoleptic, prone to sudden sleep-fits, but, for some reason, I thought about felines. Cats sleep sixteen hours a day, popping awake and passing out without much preliminary fuss. How did that mold their perceptions? Each period of wakefulness must seem like a brand-new beginning. They must have their own internal calendars where temporal units aren't defined by the movement of the sun, rather by their urges to prowl around, then nap. Each human "day" must comprise several cat-fragment days.

Maybe, I was turning into a cat person.

A cat that was afraid of heights.

I was still alone in the belfry, which was good in a way, because it meant I really was starting to recover hidden bits of my existence. In another way, it was sad because it would have been nice to have a companion, another sleepy amnesiac who felt compelled to climb a bell tower. I removed several pieces of tattered wooden lattice obscuring the view and leaned them against one of the parapet walls. Then, I could easily see Balsam Street, the row of shops that included the bakery and pharmacy, and the parkette beside the river.

As I watched, the surface of the water started to ripple in numerous places, as if fish were surfacing to feed. I strained to look closer and saw the agitations were centered around black tree branches protruding from the water. I realized there was no nighttime fish-feeding frenzy, rather, the tree branches were vibrating.

A wisp of white mist rose above one branch tip and swirled,

forming a funnel. Another plume of mist rose from a second branch tip, and then another and another. Soon the water was completely obscured by a thick fog and I realized those "branches" were really a series of interconnected pipes.

Hidden machinery must be producing the effluent and it immediately struck me as a colossal waste of effort. If this were some sort of pesticide intended to fog the soy field, it was extremely inefficient because the mist just roiled over the calm water, a burgeoning cloud layer, twenty or thirty feet thick.

Then, a peculiar humming noise captured my attention.

The blade assemblies on the wind turbines were all slowly migrating downwards on their stalks. The giant blades dropped lower and lower until the tips just cleared the soybean plants. The blade housings also tilted forward slightly, and propellors almost clipped the tower bases. The blades looked larger, too, as if each one had slightly changed its orientation in the hub.

The humming noise increased and the turbine blades started to spin faster. That was a strange sight, because ultra-slow rotation at the top of a metal stalk had seemed so natural. I thought this unusual speed would shake the machines to pieces, but they didn't show any strain. Within a couple of minutes, I could no longer see individual blades, their movement was a visual blur like a household fan.

The river fog bent forward in the artificial wind and crawled towards the community. The fog climbed up the shallow bank, marched across the parkette and obscured the road. I could see the pipes protruding from the water again. The nozzles were spewing out streams of thick mist that twirled together to knit an opaque, rippling blanket.

The fog eddied when it encountered walls and windows but didn't significantly slow down. The mist wrapped around buildings to fill yards and alleyways, but it also seemed to penetrate brick and siding.

From my perch, I could see white swirls within bedroom windows above the various shops. The fog rolled forward, filling every crevice and depression.

I heard a dog bark, as if it had woken to find a stranger walking towards its bed, but it was just one single exclamation. After that solitary noise the community was absolutely quiet. There were no voices, no hurried footsteps, no slamming doors or windows.

The squirrels had stopped chattering and the birds were silent as well, though they continued to move in cloudlike masses that occasionally obscured the moon.

The fog crept around the corner of the library and crawled down Alder, Catalpa and Dogwood, closer and closer to the Anglican Church where I was hiding.

Within fifteen minutes, the smoky tendrils had reached Larch Street and were walking up the front steps of my sanctuary like they were eager to attend a service. I opened the trap door, looked down and saw the fog squeeze through the wooden entry doors like water penetrating coarse sand. The fog looked up at me, through the entrails of the steeple, and several snakeheads climbed towards the belfry. But the fog seemed to lose heart as it ascended the twisting spiral staircase, just below my bedroom-platform. The fog snuffled at the trap door opening, then retreated to march through the nave and explore the transepts. I slammed the trap closed again and looked through the Western tower opening. Fog streamed through minute gaps in the stained-glass windows, and jogged across the grass towards a small cluster of bungalows on the other side of a baseball diamond.

I rubbed my eyes and suddenly felt very tired. The fog must have a high specific density, I thought, a quality that prevented it from climbing higher than an Anglican bell tower. I turned around and saw a few tiny, smiling coils of smoke playing in my nest.

I don't remember lying down.

2

When I woke, tangled in my sleeping bag, the fog seemed like an element of a dream. I looked towards the river and saw the wind turbine blades slowly turning at the very tops of their metal stalks as they were supposed to.

But I could also clearly see the network of black nozzles poking above the river's placid surface. I felt silly now for ever thinking they were tree branches because it was so obvious the protrusions were uniform and mechanical.

A few people were limping through the parkette, carrying folded lawn chairs and magazines, or holding dog leashes. I opened my little toiletry bag and brushed my teeth. Maybe later, I would use the apartment on Walnut Street to take a shower. I checked my pockets to make sure I still had my glasses and magic credit card. I wasn't particularly hungry, but I thought it would be delightful to get a coffee and Danish at the bakery.

I put the glasses on and looked at my card. The same mug shot stared back at me, but below that, was a surprising name:

Orland Kurtenbach.

Jesus fuck, I had a new name, and my ID had been switched while I slept.

Think, think.

I had pulled the ladder into the tower, so I could use it to reach the spiral staircase. So, someone had dragged an additional ladder into the church yard to breach my defenses. Then they had clambered up the metal spiral staircase and popped open the trap door right beside my head. They had frisked me, and swapped ID cards all without waking me up. That seemed ridiculous, even to the paranoid fragments of my personality. But if someone hadn't physically exchanged my card, the bit of plastic had the capacity to alter itself.

I examined the card more closely. It was very thin, but I now suspected its thinness contained microscopic pipes and machinery, a miniature version of the apparatus beneath the river surface.

At any rate, I was glad to see I was still one hundred and

eighty-five centimeters tall with grey eyes. I hadn't aged further, which was comforting, still forty-one years old. And, apparently, I was still welcome at nine Walnut Street, because the home address hadn't changed.

I descended the spiral staircase and squeezed onto the top rung of the borrowed wooden ladder. Climbing down, I felt the same twinges of vertigo because the two distinct floors of empty space below kept pulsing. But I reached the bottom rung safely.

Then I maneuvered the ladder through the flapping window plastic. I jammed the ladder feet into the grass so they wouldn't slip as I descended, but it was a pretty shaky trip, never-the-less. I examined the ground and discovered a pattern of indentations but that didn't mean someone had followed me up the tower, I might have made the dents myself on earlier visits.

The air smelled different. The new aroma was very subtle, like a damp sidewalk drying in the sun. Of course, I assumed I was smelling lingering bits of night-fog, but that may have been more paranoia.

I lifted the ladder back over the neighbor's fence and let it clatter into place on support hooks. My theft was hidden by a garden shed and a couple of large forsythia bushes, but I still worried about an angry encounter with the owner.

As I walked down Alder Street, I saw a woman pouring sunflower seeds into a bird feeder. She waved at me and said, "Good morning, Orland." I waved back, with a smile frozen on my face.

I was a little nervous when I walked into the bakery. I didn't greet the man behind the counter until I was close enough to see his name tag.

Kyle had changed identities as well.

The little plastic clip attached to his shirt pocket announced he was now Kasci.

"Hey, Kasci," I said, hoping I was pronouncing it right.

"Hey, Ched."

Who the fuck was Ched?

"You want the usual?"

"Sure." I wondered what my new usual would be. The man turned around and started to toast an English Muffin. I decided to risk a delicate question. "Hey Kasci…" The man looked over his shoulder but his hands continued to fuss with breakfast ingredients. "How the hell did I ever get the nickname Ched?"

Kasci-Kyle-Whatever chuckled softly. "Oh, that was ages ago. You don't remember? You got that haircut with shaved sides and a flat top. It looked like someone gave you a wedge of soft cheese to wear as a hat, with the pointy end facing your nose. So, everyone called you Cheese-Head for a while." I smelled cream cheese and jam. "Then someone adjusted it to Cheddar-Head." He looked up at the exhaust fan. "I can't remember who started that. Anyway, after a while, Cheddar-Head got shortened to Ched once your hair grew back."

"Oh yeah." What a strange conversation. Kasci calmly accepted that I didn't know the derivation of my own nickname, he didn't balk at the mini history lesson. One of my paranoid brain fragments wondered if Kasci had been reprogrammed in the same manner as my ID card. If so, the data dump was extensive, including a stock of trivial anecdotes about customers.

It was strange to stand there, surrounded by pleasant smells, and speculate the person preparing your breakfast had been thoroughly brainwashed by a night fog.

I scratched the stubble under my chin.

Fuck it, there had to be a less-crazy explanation. Kasci wasn't some cyborg or puppet, he was a human, and human brains can't be emptied and re-filled like kitchen cannisters.

On the other hand, Kasci's anecdote about my supposed nickname was delivered in a very robotic manner. One of the paranoid fragments of my personality warned me against making glib assumptions.

I squeezed my eyes shut.

No, my first impression was right, Kasci was very human. He had a patch of dry skin on his neck, and his shoes were worn on the instep edge, evidence of bad pronation when he walked. His little fingers were curled with arthritis and he was missing a tooth.

The paranoid fragment of my brain pointed out that any artisan able to create a pastry-baking robot could just as easily make a pastry-baking robot with lots of superficial imperfections.

But why would someone work from a defective template? Wouldn't you want something that had all its teeth and a normal gait?

"Here you go." Kasci turned around and presented me with

four slices of English muffin, layered with multicoloured jam and cheese, along with a take-out coffee. He smiled at me and his missing canine was like a gap in a wall.

I carried my meal across the street to the parkette.

There was a lawn chair set up in the exact same place where I had napped yesterday. I stood behind it, juggling my English muffins and coffee. A few people were strolling along the riverbank, but absolutely no one was close enough to exert ownership over the chair. I touched the aluminum rails. No dew. At the far edge of the parkette, a man in an orange jumpsuit was cutting grass with a push-lawnmower. I think it was the same employee who waved at me yesterday.

I sat down, ate, and sipped at my coffee. There were no fishermen in the park today, but maybe they would show up later in the afternoon.

I may have nodded off because my coffee was suddenly cold when I took a sip.

"You've certainly picked a beautiful spot to sit."

I looked up and saw the same lady who had talked to me yesterday. She greeted me using almost the exact same words but this time, she had a newspaper tucked under her arm instead of a lawn chair and she had a subtle British accent. Her "you've" was phonetically more like "yer've."

"Yes," I said. "The river is gorgeous."

"I see yer've found yer glasses."

I instinctively felt my forehead. I guess I had propped the glasses up there while in the bakery. Obviously, this lady remembered our brief encounter yesterday, but somehow, overnight, she had changed ethnicity.

The fog must have been responsible, although it was impossible to imagine how. A fog might conceivably drug people, make them forget who and where they were, it might even cause mass hallucinations. But it couldn't change a vestigial accent, or implant memories about the genesis of a bakery customer's nickname.

"The war news looks good," the lady said shifting her newspaper slightly.

"Listen," I said, "I hope you won't think this is a strange question, but are *we* allied with one particular side in the war?"

"Of course," she replied. "The Nigerians."

"Okay. Thanks. It's just that I've been having these bouts of amnesia lately." I winced and the reading glasses slipped off my forehead onto my nose. The movement surprised me, but it lightened the announcement of my disability. The woman and I both laughed. "Frankly, I've been losing a lot more than my glasses."

"Don't worry about it, dearie, everyone in the Enclave is recovering from something."

I nodded. "What are you recovering from?"

"A broken 'art," she said, then laughed loudly. "No, seriously, I hurt my leg at work. I was almost crushed by a roll of newsprint." She paused. "I'm Elinore. You're Orland."

I nodded. I didn't bother mentioning that some people called me 'Ched.' "Is this a hospital?" I waved with the hand that wasn't holding a cold coffee, trying to include the entire community.

"Well…" Elinore didn't like the label. "It's like a convalescent *ward* of a hospital."

My mind called up images of wounded WWI soldiers lounging on the grounds of spa-like hotels. I wasn't sure if it was a scene I'd actually witnessed or proxy-memory from reading a book or watching a movie. But I seized on the idea of a cultured, aristocratic recovery space. "Are there any doctors around?"

Elinore scrunched up her lips. "There's Doctor Crecy at the pharmacy. He has the authority to prescribe pills. *He's* a doctor." Apparently, Doctor Crecy's name hadn't changed overnight. "There's a paramedic at the firehall to deal with minor injuries." She shifted her hips. "If you're taken ill, I mean seriously ill, an ambulance will come and fetch you. The hospital is outside the walls. But, I don't think it's too far away, though."

"Maybe I'll see Doctor Crecy," I lied, "and try to get a handle on these memory lapses." Internally, I realized no trustworthy doctor would sanction the type of manipulation I was witnessing. Sure, making someone speak with a different accent on different days was essentially harmless, but it was still unethical. A doctor who would tolerate *that* was liable to tolerate anything. But, maybe, I could trick the man into prescribing some stimulants so I could stay awake long enough to figure out what was going on.

Who knows, with the proper medication, I might even work up the energy to walk the circumference of the wall.

"I live in those bungalows, by the dam." Elinore pointed at

the spot where the wall traversed the river.

"It's a lovely wall," I said.

"Yes, isn't it. We've got no complaints, there. Where do you live?"

"Nine Walnut Street. Upper, rear."

Just then, a small bulldog clambered up the riverbank and bounded towards us, trailing a leash. Maybe 'bounded' is the wrong word. The animal had lots of enthusiasm but he seemed a little arthritic. It was the same dog the lady had yesterday. The bulldog sniffed my pantlegs then bounced his front paws onto my right knee, so I could scratch his ears. I looked at the tag swinging below his jowls. It identified the animal as "Cecil." Yesterday, he had been called "Kazimir."

The woman took a couple of limping steps toward the bungalows. "C'mon, Cecil," she said, "it's time for yer breakfast." The dog instantly flounced after her.

The animal recognized its new name.

If this Enclave was an elaborate conspiracy designed for the sole purpose of confusing me, the dog was in on it. I watched them wobble past the empty parking platform to the little row of bungalows at the river's edge.

I put my English Muffin wrapper in the same garbage container I used yesterday. When I peeked inside the metal cylinder, I saw a stained piece of carpet and a few yards of rope.

I needed more help decoding this community. Everyone who talked to me was friendly and helpful, but they weren't exactly reliable. Elinore and Kasci seemed to be victims of manipulation, just like me. But their situations were arguably worse, because they weren't even aware their leashes were being tugged.

Maybe I should start my journey of understanding with a little light reading. I could get a couple of newspapers or a book and perhaps get a better handle on what was considered "normal" in my new world. I skipped across the street and pushed the PharmaSave door open. Kelly was in the make-up aisle loading bottles of moisturizer onto a shelf. She looked up as I entered and said "Hi Al..." Her voice froze and she lowered her eyebrows, pursed her lips, then amended the greeting. "I mean Orland." She shook her head. "I'm sorry, I was up late last night watching the meteor shower. I'm still half-asleep."

The paranoid fragment of my brain gave a triumphant cheer. An actor in this farce had made a mistake and called me by yesterday's name. The whole contrivance was fragile, and could be broken if I remained strong and resolute. But the reasonable part of my brain refused to celebrate, it suspected there was a different explanation.

"Where were you," I asked, "when you watched the meteors?"

"Oh, I climbed up on my roof." Kelly yawned. "The meteors didn't show until an hour after they were supposed to, almost three a.m., but I forced myself to stay awake."

"I would have thought it was too foggy to see anything, last night."

"Oh, no. There was a lot of low-lying mist from the river, around midnight, but that's nothing new. The sky was clear."

Kelly and I had both done the same thing last night, for different reasons. I had climbed the Anglican Church steeple tower, following the lead of birds and squirrels who seemed to be hellbent on getting as far away from the ground as possible. Kelly had elevated herself to get a better look at some pretty nighttime sparks. But the net effect was the same. Our short-term memories weren't quite wiped clean.

True, Kelly had only blurted out the first syllable of my yesterday-name, while I was aware of comprehensive, cross-species reprogramming. But, then again, I had occupied the very highest point in our community, Kelly's rooftop wasn't quite as lofty.

My eyes pivoted to the dispensary at the back of the store. Dr. Crecy's name was still printed blue-on-blue on the bulkhead. The pharmacist had his mini binoculars on once again and he was carefully crushing a substance with an old-fashioned pestle. He seemed completely absorbed in his task.

My eyes shifted to the name tag pinned just underneath the collar of Kelly's pharmacy smock.

Kathy.

Kelly was now named Kathy and I felt a sudden spasm of anger. My community's ID cards, employee badges and even dog tags must be miniature display screens capable of remote programming. And those changes were accompanied by a mechanically generated, memory-altering fog. But what was the endpoint of all that sophisticated effort? The exchange of one two-syllable name with another. The switch was incredibly trivial, and that made it seem perverse.

"Kathy," I said, and she looked up at me like a dog who hears a familiar collection of phonemes. "When do you finish work?"

"At one o'clock. I'm doing mornings this week."

"Would you like to go for a walk after work?"

"Sure." She nodded eagerly.

It was unkind of me, but I imagined her reaction was similar to Cecil's when Elinore jangled his leash this morning.

"How about I meet you in the park?" she suggested.

"That would be good. I want to read a couple of newspapers."

Kathy went behind the periodical counter and held up a *New York Times* issue. "This one?"

"Yes. And let me have one of those *Ttupak Enclaves,* as well." May as well face the local propaganda, head on. There was a shelf of paperback novels, including *The Eight-Kitten Christmas,* but I resisted.

Kathy scanned my card and smiled as she handed me the newspapers. "The war news looks good."

"Yeah. Listen Kathy, I hope this doesn't sound like a weird question, but I've had these strange memory lapses the past few days, where I lose track of what's going on around me...who are we allied with in this war?"

"Oh, don't be embarrassed, recovery isn't a straight path, there are lots of twists and turns."

"Okay, I get that. So, who are we allied with?"

"The Indians, of course." She smiled again. "I'll see you a few minutes after one."

"Thank you."

Look both ways. No traffic except for a wheeled cart the maintenance guy in orange coveralls was pushing along the street. He occasionally bent down to pick up a twig or a piece of fluff. The pavement was spotless.

The lawn chair where I ate breakfast was still available, so I flopped down and unfolded the *Times*. There was a picture of the Perseid meteor shower accompanying a brief article. Apparently, it was the longest, brightest appearance in more than two centuries. The article mentioned the phenomenon was best observed at two a.m. in the Midwest, and three a.m. nearer the Eastern Seaboard.

That information made me happy, because the paranoid slivers of my brain had previously speculated the pharmacy's stock of newspapers was as phony as the rest of the town, just meant to prop up the residents' delusions. But if the newspapers accurately reported events you could witness with your own eyes, like a meteor shower, there was hope I might be able to figure out what was objectively true and separate it from what was staged and what was produced by my own imagination.

There were more front-page articles about the war, but no specific battles were described. An Indian general had been assassinated by a "Vespula," which seemed to be an insect-like drone. There was speculation the killing might actually help peace negotiations because the dead general had been very keen to pursue a perceived advantage. His successor might be more generous-minded.

That account didn't quite square with yesterday's news that Nigerians were massing on the Andaman Islands, preparing for an attack on Madras.

The Surgeon General was still promising to do something about the agricultural worker shortage, without offering an identifiable strategy.

There were two articles about a "Tanit" shortage. I eventually figured out Tanit was a synthetic element used in micro-miniature batteries. As I understood it, Tanit enabled long-range drone attacks like the one that killed the Indian general. The element must have been important in household micro-circuitry as well, because one article blamed the shortage for crippling supply chain issues in the manufacture of TVs, home computers and phones.

My fingers flexed, crumpling the newsprint.

Until the article mentioned TVs, computers and phones I had completely forgotten those things existed. I had experienced a number of fragmented memories of books and movies, but nothing about those other technologies. I hadn't even noticed that my tiny apartment on Walnut Street didn't contain a phone or a TV set. Once those devices were mentioned, I remembered they were important and ubiquitous but, at the same time, I couldn't dredge up a single memory of personal interaction with them.

I abandoned the *Times* and switched to the *Ttupak Enclave*.

As I had suspected yesterday, this "newspaper" was really just an amateurish information sheet about the community. It was formatted like the front section of the *Times,* but there was no date underneath the banner. That led me to believe I was holding the one and only edition.

The Enclave was established near Oberlin, Kansas (again, no date given) by two doctors named Decimattu and Arakpak. It was initially intended as an "overflow" institution to take the pressure off a strained health-care system. Residents of the Enclave needed some support, but not a lot of traditional medical intervention. Residents could be monitored electronically and would care for each other in a "commune" model, with arms-length supervision.

The Ttupak Enclave was intended to be a template for a series of future healing centers, a distinct layer in a forward-looking, comprehensive health care system.

Perhaps, the electronic "monitoring" of patients had morphed into more sophisticated manipulation, like the identity shifts I had witnessed.

There was a large photograph of the founders. Doctor Decimattu was a youngish woman with dark ringlets who looked like she had borrowed a pair of Doctor Arakpak's glasses for dress up day. Dr. Arakpak looked more like a conventional doctor, an elderly guy with bad posture and a stethoscope swinging from his neck. He was holding a clipboard.

A small sliver of my brain suspected Dr. Decimattu was Nigerian and Dr. Arakpak was Indian.

I fell asleep reading the *New York Times* "Ethicist" column. The letter-writer asked if it was okay to lie about something fairly trivial to avoid hurting a friend's feelings. The answer extolled the importance of "honesty" as the glue that holds society together, but admitted there were certain exceptional circumstances where lying was ethically permissible. I had difficulty following the argument because I was distracted by the fundamental dishonesty of paved roads and parking lots in a community without cars.

Kathy woke me by gently shaking my shoulder. I got the impression people in the Enclave made appointments then fell asleep all the time. Kathy didn't think it was worth mentioning.

I climbed out of the lawn chair and rubbed my eyes. "Where did you want to walk?" I asked. I was hoping she would suggest taking a closer look at the wall.

"I'd like to see your apartment. Mine's a little small. The houses on Walnut Street look bigger."

"I don't know who owns this lawn chair," I said.

"It probably belongs to the Enclave. I see maintenance people collecting them all the time. Don't worry about it." We walked across the grass to Balsam Street. I tucked the newspapers under my arm because I wanted something to fidget with.

I noticed Kathy took a careful look in both directions before we crossed the street. "It's a tough habit to break," I said, "checking for traffic."

Kathy's mouth turned into a pinprick, like she was considering the issue for the first time. "I guess." But she tried to defend the practice. "Sometimes the maintenance staff use electric vehicles. Those things are pretty quiet, so you have to be careful."

We started walking down Alder and Kathy waved at someone through the PharmaSave window. "Where are you from?" I asked.

"A little town called Fort Scott."

"Kansas?"

"Yeah."

"What is it like?"

She took a noisy breath. "It's a lot like here. Small, but older. There's an historical district where all the buildings have plaques and the streets have this bright orange brick instead of pavement. And the geography is a little flatter. Here, everything rolls, slightly." Her hand made a snake-like motion through the air. Apparently, that's all there was to say about Fort Scott. "Where are you from?" she asked.

"I don't have any idea."

"Oh." Kathy didn't find that any more troubling than the spontaneous naps. "We get that a lot here." She reached up and squeezed my tricep. "You just have to be patient."

The casual physical contact made me surprisingly sad. Perhaps it was a reminder of how pleasant life could be in different circumstances. "Patient? I've been here for ages and every time I wake up it's my first day all over again." I had no idea how long I had been in the Enclave, and I hated to be disingenuous, but I needed to prompt Kathy to talk.

"Oh, you've only been here a few months." The tricep got another squeeze. "Head injuries are complicated. I've seen people take…" She paused, not wanting to make my situation seem too bleak. "…a lot longer and still have everything work out fine."

I wondered if Kathy had access to my medical files. "How long have you worked in the Enclave?"

"Four years?" She stopped walking and crossed her arms. "No, five years. I was an educational assistant in Fort Scott, when I was recruited." We started walking again.

"Can I see your ID card?"

"Sure." Kathy stuck a hand into her pocket and extracted the bit of plastic. She handed it to me without the slightest hesitation.

There was something disconcerting about her friendliness and cooperation. If I asked her to take her clothes off, arch backwards and crabwalk down the street, she might say "sure," with the exact same tone of voice and start disrobing.

I was looking for someone I could trust, not someone I could trust until another person intruded.

I looked at the card. The young woman's name was Kathy Anderson and she was 164 centimeters tall. She lived at six Alder Street, upper front. Her card looked slightly different than mine, hers had a stamp on the back, something that looked like a postage cancellation mark, except it was integrated into the plastic, not an ink overlay.

I was happy to see she was thirty-four years old. She looked a lot younger than that, partly because she was small. I had experienced a sudden sexual re-awakening when Kathy touched my arm and one of the paranoid slivers of my brain had sent an immediate warning signal about lusting after someone who was too young to be a suitable playmate. Since Kathy was thirty-four, I could probably tell that section of my brain to fuck off and mind its own business.

Kathy looked from side to side as we walked the alphabet towards Walnut Street, as if she rarely visited this section of her tiny community. We went to the back of number nine and climbed the stairs. We didn't see any of the other tenants and Kathy didn't ask who they were.

I unlocked the door and Kathy said "Oh, *yeah*." Her hands were on her hips and her head tilted back. "This is *nice*."

Context is everything. To me, the apartment was a prison cell.

"Why don't you have any photographs?" she asked, looking at

the bare walls and tabletop.

"I don't know. Like I said, I've been struggling with these bouts of amnesia. You could put some random picture in a frame, tell me it's my grandma and I wouldn't know the difference."

"That's so sad. I've got pictures of my parents and my sister and a dog I had when I was a kid." Her eyes almost closed. "My sister's holding a little trophy she got for the 'Iron Stomach Award' at the fall fair." Kathy tilted her head and looked up at me through her eye slits. "I could speak to Dr. Crecy. He could arrange to have some mementos delivered. That might help the memory issues."

"Photos wouldn't help," I said. "I wouldn't know if I was experiencing real memories, or something whipped up to match the photos."

"You'd *feel* it. If the memories were real, deep down, you'd know."

"I'm not sure. The disconnect is pretty deep." I rubbed my forehead. Simply talking with another human-being made me feel a lot better. Maybe I was whining about something that would self-correct after a couple more blueberry pastries and a few arm-squeezes.

"How do you know *your* pictures are real?" I asked.

Kathy wasn't offended by the question. "Oh, there's layer after layer of emotional corroboration." She smiled. "There's one picture of me climbing out the window of a demolition derby car…"

"You drove in demolition derbies?"

"All the seniors in our high school did. It was our big fall tech project. We moved the gas tanks into the back seats so they wouldn't explode. We took out the window glass, put in debris netting and welded safety cages." She showed me a red welt on the inside of her elbow, the obvious residue of an orthopedic intervention. "I still managed to break my arm taking out Bobby Bare in his Galaxy five hundred. That thing was like a tank. I had him pinned against the concrete barriers and he almost climbed into my Parisienne."

In a way, Kathy's reminiscences had the same stagey quality as Kasci's anecdote about my nickname "Ched." But her voice was passionate and that made me reluctant to accuse her of parroting some ghost-written narrative.

"So, one thing leads to another."

"Reality is a constellation of things." She grabbed my arm again. "Like the smell of hay on a farm." Her left eye narrowed. "Have you ever been in a bird barn?"

"I don't know."

"If you had, you'd know it. The sensation is visceral. The blast of warmth when you open the door, the coolness in your throat from ammonia released by manure. The smell of resin as the wood chip bedding dries out. And there's disinfectant in the air too, a weird medicinal smell that seeps out of the walls after fumigation. You can even smell the electrical wires as they heat up and activate the feed machines."

"Hmmm." Was it possible to have false memories of smells? It seemed unlikely.

Then I experienced another spasm of paranoia, because Kasci had talked about my Cheddar-head haircut as if we'd shared child-hoods, but that wasn't possible if I had only been in the Enclave for a few months.

But maybe Kasci was just being kind, recounting a familiar story in order to humor a brain-damaged customer.

I had to admit, a profound head injury was the most likely explanation for my strange experiences in the Enclave. The sud-den name changes, transforming ID cards, evil fogs, and uncon-trolled naps could all be by-products of that damage. Maybe all it took to imagine a vast conspiracy was a tiny swelling of cortical tissue or a minute decrease in blood flow. A period of rest and recovery might allow the craziness to dissipate, like a night fog.

Of course, if the injury was catastrophic, I was doomed to bake up a new batch of delusions each morning. Every day, I would select a new recipe and start mixing ingredients, carefully kneading in fresh nuggets of bullshit. I might even imagine that other people corroborated my nonsense. If that were the case, there was no dependable foundation. If I could imagine people chatting about an eighty-foot wall with a decorative scalloped top, I could easily invent the wall itself.

Maybe, employees in this strange convalescent community were instructed to squeeze my arm, and go for walks, and talk about how I was getting better when, really, I was chasing my own tail.

The "head injury" scenario made a lot of sense because it was mathematically simple. If a problem resided solely within one dented brain, then hordes of people didn't have to cooperatively lie, minute after minute, day after day, to maintain a bizarre conspiracy.

The only thing arguing against that theory was my open-mindedness. I had a feeling that truly delusional people were more stubborn, that they clung to their fixations with more passion.

I was interested in the truth. I wanted someone to share an experience so I could verify it really happened. When Kathy bobbled my name, then talked about climbing on a roof to watch the heavens, I latched onto her like a lamprey because we seemed to be swimming in the same direction.

"Are you sure you live here?" Kathy had wandered into the bathroom and must have noticed the emptiness, like I did yesterday. "I mean, I saw your card unlock the door, but you don't have very much stuff."

"I think I've moved out."

Kathy came back into the living area. She seemed puzzled, but she was also smiling. I had intrigued her. "Where did you move?"

"I'll show you."

"Okay."

When we walked to the front of the house, we saw one of my fellow tenants swiping his card to open the front door. He greeted me by name: "Hello Orland."

I didn't know who he was, but Kathy rescued me. "Hey, Raymond." I guess, he was a customer at the PharmaSave. "We just got a new batch of that moisturizer in."

"Good."

"Would you like me to leave a tube in your mailbox?"

"Thanks, that would be great." Raymond nodded twice then shuffled into the hall. The man didn't look inordinately busy, why couldn't he pick up his own moisturizer? What an ass.

On the other hand, I was happy to hear about the delivery service because it helped explain why everyone in this tiny community had a mailbox.

It occurred to me Kathy must have seen every Enclave resident at some time or another, in the PharmaSave. Of course, she mentioned we hadn't talked prior to our meeting yesterday, even though I'd been in the Enclave for several months. I suppose, if identities were regularly changed, she wouldn't really get to *know* anyone, she would just recognize the data markers clinging to their husks.

I wondered if the fog distributed that data. Perhaps, tiny airborne storage particles were ingested by sleeping residents, then those particles migrated to the memory centres of the brain.

Of course, I was operating on the assumption I *wasn't* barking mad and imagining the entirety of my experience in the Enclave. I told myself there was nothing wrong with exploring alternative possibilities as long as I kept an open mind and didn't handcuff myself to any one crazy theory.

Maybe every resident was micro-chipped like a house pet, and the fog triggered programming that was already in place.

Offhand, I couldn't see any value in that type of extensive mind control. It wasn't as if the residents were being encouraged to produce more widgits for the war effort. As far as I could tell, the Enclave was full of people who didn't give a shit, then took a nap.

It was even crazier to manipulate pets like Cecil or Enclave staff, like Kathy. Dogs have already demonstrated they can be endlessly manipulated. They exchanged their souls for liver-flavoured-treats thousands of years ago. And you'd think it would be helpful to have a few clear-headed employees just to manage infrastructure concerns, like making sure the water supply was potable and Raymond got the proper moisturizer.

Fuck it.

I'd only been awake for two days. I needed more time to make sense of things.

Kathy and I walked past the beautifully maintained baseball diamond I had observed yesterday. "Do people actually use that ballpark?" I waved at the field.

"Not a lot. We have fun games occasionally, and picnics. There's not a league, or anything." She took a breath. "The demographic doesn't lend itself to intense physical activity."

"Yeah." I imagined the elderly fisherman sliding into second base. His body would shatter under the weight of a forceful tag. "I'll bet you're a good baseball player," I said. It seemed like a reasonable inference for someone raised in the mid-west, someone who built her own demolition derby car in high school.

"Oh yeah, I always get the hot-corner when we play."

This is a difficult thing to describe, but Kathy's voice sounded wrong. I mean, there was an element of pride in her ability, and even joy at the prospect of playing baseball, but it was different than when she described the smells inside a barn. *That* sounded sincere.

"The helicopter uses the field as a landing pad, too."

I was glad to hear Kathy mention modern machinery. I'd seen maintenance people wheeling carts down the street and cutting lawns with push-mowers. When Elinore mentioned an "ambulance" I half-expected it to be a horse-drawn buggy. "What does the helicopter do?"

"It's an air ambulance," Kathy said. She pursed her lips and seemed to be really thinking about it for the first time. "But it delivers supplies, too."

"This way." I tugged Kathy's arm, guiding her down Larch Street to the side lawn of the Anglican church. I reached over the neighbor's fence and pulled the rickety wooden ladder off its hooks. Then I leaned it against the window that was covered with flapping plastic.

"You live in the steeple tower? Neat." Kathy climbed up the rungs like a ring-tailed lemur.

"Careful," I called after her, "the stairway's been pulled out of the lower stories." When I poked my head through the plastic, I saw Kathy standing on the narrow ledge, examining the brick-work. She obviously didn't share my fear of heights. Her toes hung over the edge and she leaned forward to look at the church floor, below.

I pulled the ladder through the window opening and jammed it against the opposite wall. Kathy jumped on it and started climbing before I could make any paranoid adjustments. She slipped between the brick wall and metal spiral staircase, and I heard her footsteps make *ting ting ting* noises like a cat playing with its water dish. I lumbered in her wake. Once, I looked down between the ladder rungs and saw empty space swell and shrink like an invisible monster. I had to deliberately re-focus on my hand grips.

I climbed the spiral stairs to the belfry and pulled myself through the trap door opening.

Kathy had her hands on her hips, and she was slowly rotating, taking in the entirety of the view. "I love it up here." I thought her voice held genuine enthusiasm. She reached out, grabbed my hand, and I joined the fresh examination of her world.

Unfortunately, the handholding didn't feel like a romantic gesture, more like a teenager taking a younger sibling to the fall fair and trying to make sure he didn't get lost. She abruptly let go after we'd made two circuits.

"What's the purpose of the wall," I asked. A portion of the scalloped top was visible to the west.

"Well…"

Something de-railed her response. Her face darkened, and I was terrified my curiosity had triggered some sort of seizure. I imagined a diabolical implant was monitoring Kathy's thoughts and the device was set to explode if she came close to divulging the Enclave's secrets.

Of course, she may just have been embarrassed she couldn't answer a simple question.

"What's on the other side of the wall?" I quickly amended the inquiry.

Kathy's face cleared and she took a deep breath. "I hear there's a military base in the area, where they train drone pilots. And there's lots of Greenhouses. It's a big farming district."

I remembered seeing a flash of light outside the wall, last evening. It could have been sunlight reflecting off glass roofs.

"Hey, you brought your SuppleTee with you." Kathy pointed at the toiletries next to my balled up sleeping bag.

"What's Subtlety?"

"SuppleTee," she corrected me. "We move tons of that stuff at the PharmaSave. I use the peach blend, myself."

I looked at the wrinkled tube. Apparently, in my Allan Ripke iteration, I valued soft skin. For some reason, that knowledge made me feel uncomfortable. Maybe I didn't fully trust my own alter-ego. I deftly switched the topic to last night's Perseids Shower by showing Kathy the write up in today's Times.

She read the article and nodded her head several times and said the shower was definitely worth staying up for.

That meteor shower was ointment for my chipped and dented brain. It was a bit of undeniable, external reality. "But what about this?" I pointed to the section that described the best viewing times across the continental United States. "You said the meteor shower didn't start until almost three a.m."

"Right." Kathy nodded. She still didn't see it.

"You expected to see it at *two,* because that's when the paper said it would be visible over the Midwest."

Her brows furrowed. "It was delayed."

"By what? Intergalactic traffic? Bad weather?"

Kathy laughed. "You're right, that's ridiculous." She looked at me. "What do *you* think it means?"

"We're not in Kansas anymore."

"What?" She was still confused.

"I read that little monograph about the founding of the Ttupak Enclave. It said we're located near Oberlin."

"Right."

"Is that anywhere near Fort Scott?"

"No. Oberlin is way up north, near Nebraska. Fort Scott is almost in Missouri."

"Okay." The geography lesson was a dangerous distraction. I would have to hurry or I would lose my focus completely. "Anyway, if we were actually near Oberlin, you would have seen the Perseids at two a.m. But you didn't see them until three, so we're not in Kansas. We're closer to the Eastern Seaboard."

"That's very clever." Kathy smiled like I had pulled a quarter out of her ear at a birthday party. "But why would anyone…"

"Earlier this morning, you almost called me Allan. Why did you do that?"

She sighed. "I screwed up. I see a lot of people."

"No. That really was my name, at least the name on my ID card, yesterday."

Kathy narrowed her eyes. "Your ID card changed?"

"Yes."

Kathy turned away and did another slow-turning survey of the Enclave.

"I know it sounds crazy," I said, "but that isn't the craziest thing that happened last night, not by a long shot. But you could help me out, if you stayed here this evening and…"

"…verified." She seemed to understand.

"Yes. I'd like to stay up late again, look at the Enclave from this bell tower, and tell you everything I see."

"And I'll tell you if you're hallucinating or not." She stuck out a hand. "Deal."

The incidental physical contact made me feel happy for a fraction of a second, then I noticed her opaque white fingernails. I don't know why I didn't see it earlier.

"What's the matter?" she said. My face must have registered the shock I felt.

"Your fingernails were bright pink yesterday." I held her hand like it was a dying fish.

Kathy laughed. "I re-did them, just as my shift ended. I was demonstrating some products for a couple of ladies."

"Oh."

"Did you think my body was changing, like your ID card?"

"Yes," I admitted sadly. I suddenly felt ill.

Kathy reached up and squeezed the back of my neck. "Don't worry about it. I'm happy to sit here with you tonight."

"You won't be too tired at work tomorrow?"

"I don't go in tomorrow." She hoisted her little body up and sat on the ledge of the belfry wall. I felt a spasm of proxy panic, but Kathy clearly didn't share my vertigo. "Work schedules in the Enclave aren't exactly onerous, that's partly why we all applied. I only work four-hour shifts, four days a week."

Applied? Yesterday, she said she was recruited. "Do you have a lot of hobbies?" I asked.

"Not really. I help tend a community vegetable garden. It's purely organic, no pesticides. Working there is a form of meditation, sometimes I wander through the rows for hours picking bugs off the leaves with my fingers."

I must have fallen asleep because the words "fingers, fingers, fingers," echoed in my mind and when I snapped back to attention the sky was darkening. I heard the church bell ringing softly over our heads. I looked up and a pair of red eyes stared back at me.

"It's a raccoon," Kathy said. She was sitting in a corner of the belfry, directly across from me. "He clambered up there a half hour ago."

Ting ting ting. The animal wasn't satisfied with its hiding spot inside the bell. It slid down the clapper then leapt towards the emptiness of the western opening. I felt sure the animal would plummet to his death, but he hooked a fingernail on a scrap of lattice then swung up and out of sight. We heard his claws scrape on the exterior copper sheathing as the animal worked its way to the very pinnacle. It was trying to get as high as possible, away from an impending threat.

I carefully leaned out to look at the sky directly above the steeple. A swirling cloud of sparrows formed letter shapes in the sky, but the writing was too frenzied to decode.

I felt incredibly relieved.

The whole point of luring Kathy to the bell tower was to have her witness the artificial fog blowing through the town. But logical fragments of my brain had already warned me the phenomenon wasn't likely to occur every single night. It would be hard to justify the colossal effort, if you looked at it from the point of view of the perpetrators. Perhaps the fog only appeared once a week, once a month or once a year.

But the animals sensed it was about to happen again, and that made me happy.

"Look." I summoned Kathy to the Eastern side of the tower, facing the parkette, and beyond that, the river. "Do you see the tree branches poking up through the water?"

"Yes," she said. "They're quivering."

"Now look at the wind turbines." The giant fan blades had shifted position in their hubs, and the assemblies were slowly migrating down the metal stalks towards the soy field.

I glanced at Kathy's face and she was smiling, mesmerized by the movement.

The fog streamed from the quivering nozzles in the river, piling up on itself like swirls of icing. The turbine blades slowly settled into their low position, just grazing the plants. Then the individual blades disappeared, and we heard a quiet mechanical hum, like a fan in a neighboring apartment. The river-mist somersaulted up the bank, and across the parkette. It didn't bother checking for traffic, it roiled across Balsam Street and nuzzled against the PharmaSave and bakery.

The vanguard of the fog seemed like a living thing, using appendages to touch, taste, and explore everything it encountered.

"That's my place," Kathy said as the fog enveloped a row of houses immediately behind the stores.

The fog rolled through the alphabet of tree-themed streets: Catalpa and Dogwood and Elm. It moved past the library and baseball diamond, and started to crawl up the bell tower of the Anglican church where we were hiding. We looked through the trap door as thin white fingers grasped the wooden ladder rungs, then we saw delicate fog-feet on the treads of the metal spiral staircase. A dozen ghost-like forearms reached through the opening and touched the platform at our feet.

Then the fog retreated, eager to infiltrate other spaces.

"How extraordinary," Kathy said.

3

When I woke, Kathy and I were huddled together in a corner of the bell tower, with my sleeping bag wrapped around our shoulders. She was snoring lightly, but soon woke, as if aware I was staring at her.

"Good morning," she said, then paused. Clearly, she intended to attach a name to the greeting, but had difficulty spitting it out.

"Who am I?"

Kathy's mouth shrank into a tiny nozzle opening. "Do you mind if I still call you Allan?"

"That would be fine." I shifted a hip and pulled my ID card from a pocket and looked at it. "But you'd better only call me Allan when we're alone." I held the card in the palm of my hand, hiding it, as if we were rehearsing a magic trick. "Can you tell me the name that is now printed on my ID card?"

Kathy squinted, as if recollection required an effort. "Carol Vadnais. I think that's what I'm supposed to call you, now."

I turned the card around so she could see the etched information. "You're right."

"How extraordinary." She fished her own ID card out of a pocket, looked at the name and nodded at me. "What's my name?"

"I don't have any idea." It was a sad admission. "You have grey eyes," I said, as if that mitigated my ignorance.

"Krystal Anderson." She turned the card around to show me.

"Anderson is the same last name as yesterday." I wondered why I rated a wholesale name change and she didn't.

She nodded. "You should call me Krystal, now. I remember being Kathy, yesterday, but that's wrong, somehow. I don't feel like a Kathy."

"Okay." I wondered about our differing immunity to this latest programming shift. I no longer had the excuse of climbing to a higher safe-spot, Krystal and I were siting beside each other when the fog rolled through, at the exact same elevation. Yet I was utterly ignorant of the name changes, and she seemed to be aware of both realities. "How long have I been in the Enclave, Krystal?"

I liked the sound of her new name. It was gem-like.

She stared at me. "You're a new arrival."

"I haven't been here for several months?"

"No, you were just shipped in." Krystal paused. "I know what I said yesterday, I remember our conversation, but this is, like, new." She frowned. "Come to think of it, I'm not sure which story is right."

We stood up and did a slow rotation in the bell tower, checking out the Enclave, which was physically unchanged. People were strolling through the parkette, and shore birds were flitting through the rushes along the river's edge. The wind turbines were at the top of their metal stalks, where they were supposed to be, turning with deliberate slowness.

"I'd like to take a walk along the wall," I said. "Would you come with me?"

"Sure."

The agreement was casual, just like last night's decision to crawl up a steeple tower and nest. Krystal didn't seem to fully register the enormity of what we had witnessed last night.

"Let's start at the dam," she said, "I want to get a croissant from the bakery."

"Okay." I had a sudden craving for a coffee.

We happened to pass Raymond as we walked down Alder Street. "Hello, Yuri," Krystal said.

"Hello, Krystal. Hello Carol." The response was immediate and natural.

When we entered the bakery, Krystal quickly greeted the man behind the counter to save me the trouble of examining his shifting name tag. "Hello, Stan."

"Hello." He nodded at both of us. "Krystal, Carol. The usual?"

"Sure." I wondered what the new usual would be. After a few minutes, I found out: white chocolate scones and dark coffee for me, herbal tea and a croissant for Krystal.

"You're off today?" Stan asked as he passed containers over the counter.

"Yeah." Krystal nodded.

"But Dr. Crecy will be there?"

"Yeah. He might be in his office, but just ask Wendy at the pharmacy counter, she'll fetch him for you."

"Okay." Stan rubbed the back of his neck. He obviously didn't want to talk about a medical problem in front of me. I wondered if that dry patch of skin I had noticed was bothering him.

I was eager to leave the bakery. As soon as we were on the sidewalk I pointed out "Dr. Crecy's name didn't change."

"No."

Krystal's response was matter-of-fact, she didn't see the sinister implication: if Dr. Crecy was excluded from the data manipulation, he might be the person responsible for it. I scratched the stubble underneath my chin. Of course, if Dr. Crecy wasn't reprogrammed, how would he be able to interact with his PharmaSave customers? How would he learn a thousand new names and backstories?

Krystal waved at a maintenance worker in orange coveralls. The man was raking up a tiny pile of twigs in the parkette and he paused to smile and raise a hand. It was the same person I had seen sweeping the curbs, yesterday.

We looked both ways, then crossed the deserted street.

"Hello Rachel, hello Sigismund." Krystal greeted the elderly lady I had talked to yesterday, and her little dog. Sigismund responded to his new name and hobbled towards us. We both knelt down to pet him and he happily alternated between sets of fingers scratching his ears.

"He seems exceptionally happy, today," I said, closely inspecting his dog tag. Sigismund had replaced Cecil.

The lady nodded. "He's having a goot day." Rachel had a different accent today, slightly Germanic. "Are you going for a walk?"

"Yes," I said, "we're going to walk along the wall."

"It's a lovely wall," Rachel said and Sigismund panted in agreement. "Enjoy yourselves." She limped towards the little row of cottages near the spot where wall crossed river. She was still favoring her right hip. The little bulldog speed-hobbled behind her, trailing his leash.

"Let's sit on the bank," I said, pointing to a patch of grass that sloped right to the water's edge. I flopped down and started eating the scones. They were delicious. I sipped the coffee; it was delightful.

Krystal sat down beside me and nibbled at her pastry, and pointed at an Osprey skimming the surface of the brown water, almost touching it with his wing tips. "I haven't noticed that bird, here, before."

The Osprey rose higher in the air, canted its enormous wings and switched directions. The bird suddenly dropped and made a noisy splash with his talons. As it rose into the air, we could see it had caught a large orange perch. The Osprey soared and looped, shrank to the size of a sparrow, and landed on the top of the wall, between two decorative scallops. The bird was now too far away to see clearly, but its head seemed to be moving up and down, eviscerating its catch.

"Where's the bridge?"

Krystal sipped her tea but didn't say anything.

"There must be a bridge across the river," I said. "Someone's obviously caring for that soy field, and those wind turbines must need maintenance as well. But when we were standing at the top of the steeple tower looking around, I don't recall seeing a bridge."

I could sense Krystal frowning, beside me. "You're right. The bridge must be at the other end of the enclave."

It was odd she didn't know. Like I said, the community wasn't large.

We finished our snacks and deposited our containers in the metal drum beside the parking platform. I checked out the other garbage. There was a stained pillow and three cracked flowerpots.

It was time to explore.

We strolled past the row of cottages where the wall crossed the river. Sigismund appeared at a window, barking happily at us. Almost immediately, we encountered the community garden, the place where Krystal did her volunteer farming. There were dozens of long skinny plots divided by gravel walkways and ending at the base of the wall. In the middle of the complex there was an open pavilion sheltering a group of picnic tables. People sat at the tables playing cards, and several dozen gardeners walked slowly through the rows of plants, occasionally examining flowers or pulling off yellowed leaves.

I felt a strong impulse to walk right beside the wall, to continuously touch it with my right hand, to constantly verify that it was real, but that was impossible here. We walked around the perimeter of the garden complex, then made a beeline to the wall.

We didn't encounter another obstacle for a long time. Suburban streets just ended like asphalt pens running out of ink. There were no curbs or borders, pavement just transitioned into a broad grass boulevard. There were lots of young trees growing on this boulevard, as well as the stumps of saplings that had been pruned away.

My very first impressions of the wall were confirmed by close contact. Metal stanchions, a meter wide, were anchored deeply in the ground, not resting on top of any sort of footing, and concrete panels were nested between them. Each panel was about three meters wide and nine or ten long. The colors were varied, grey, green, ochre, purple. Each surface was pock marked and streaked with a strange species of lichen that felt slippery like fish slime; but didn't rub off on my fingers. Every joint contained a smear of soft, rubbery sealant.

The sun was shining brightly and the wall absorbed its warmth.

We walked for an hour and barely talked. That didn't strike me as odd because, as I've already mentioned, Krystal was strangely, eerily compliant. We were walking along the wall, like I had suggested, and there was no need to caption the activity.

But we finally encountered an obstruction, a concrete garage that butted against the wall. There were three large vehicle doors facing the Enclave, all closed. Clean pavement disappeared under the edges of those doors and, I suspected, continued through the building to the other side of the Enclosure wall. There were no windows in the structure, but there was a skylight on the sloping metal roof.

"What's inside this garage?" I asked, but Krystal just shrugged.

"I've never walked to this end of the Enclave before."

That was ridiculous, like not bothering to check out the far end of your bedroom.

We walked around the garage and continued to stroll quietly beside the wall. Since walking was the only thing on the agenda, we covered a lot of ground. The angle of the sun had noticeably changed. Based on my observations from the top of the steeple tower, the Enclave's entire circumference was only ten or fifteen miles and half of that distance was occupied by soy plants, wind turbines and water.

We really should have reached the river by now.

I looked as far ahead as I could, searching for a telltale patch of bare sky, and tried to sense a slight downward slope.

"Hey," Krystal said, "we're back." She pointed at the long skinny plots of the community garden.

I looked down and saw the fingers of my *left* hand were now brushing the concrete surface of the wall, not my right. Somehow, we had switched directions and backtracked, without even realizing it had happened.

4

I was suddenly back in my nest, at the top of the steeple tower.

I must have experienced another catastrophic nap, because I couldn't remember climbing up the rickety ladder. Krystal was with me and I had the impression she had recently returned from a shift at the pharmacy. There was no obvious reason for me to think that since she wasn't wearing her smock or name tag.

To be perfectly honest, I wasn't sure how much time had elapsed since I first invited Krystal to the bell tower. We were too friendly for the newness of our acquaintance, as I imagined it. Right now, we seemed to be in the middle of an intimate conversation.

"When is the last time you remember getting angry?" I asked. To me, the strangest thing about our ineffectual walk around the Enclave was that we both quietly accepted what happened. We weren't angry or frustrated, just mildly puzzled.

Our disappointment should have been more passionate. After all, I was actively focused on our task, deliberately engaging my senses by dragging my right hand against the concrete wall, yet I couldn't pick out any specific instant where that point of contact shifted to my left.

Until, of course, we were back at the communal garden.

Our failure should have prompted an emotional outburst.

Krystal leaned back against the parapet and arched her back. She was stiff because of the unaccustomed physical activity. "I'm not sure. I remember being mad at Dr. Crecy when I thought his behavior was unprofessional." She scrunched up her face, wrestling with the timeline. "But that was a couple of years ago. Generally, life's been pretty good. Afterall, we're not in basic training, preparing to ship out to the Gangetic for a tank battle."

That must have been a reference to some war story that appeared in the news prior to my awakening. It might have happened years ago or last week, while I was getting fogged in the apartment on Walnut Street.

I scratched underneath my chin. The stubble made its usual raspy sound.

Maybe I should have shared Krystal's simple gratitude I wasn't being hustled into an incomprehensible war, but that seemed like a pretty low bar for happiness. It reminded me of the two ladies talking about our "lovely" wall, a ridiculous distraction based on some false metric of happiness.

It wasn't exactly eudaimonia.

Now, where did that word come from?

"What exactly was Dr. Crecy doing that you found offensive?" I imagined a bizarre scenario where the doctor used his medical expertise to counteract the effects of the fog and, as an added bonus, pork a bunch of vulnerable elderly ladies. But as soon as the thought popped into my consciousness, I was ashamed. It revealed more about me than it did about Dr. Crecy.

"Oh," Krystal said, "I suspected he was trying to pork a bunch of vulnerable old ladies."

I rubbed my eyes. It was impossible she would express her concern with the exact same words I used in my internal monologue, including the juvenile euphemism "pork." I must be rapidly editing reality and confusing who said or thought things.

"What did you do about it?" I had to keep the story moving forward without getting bogged down in a swamp of self-created nonsense.

"I snuck a look in his medical file."

"You had access?"

"Only temporarily. It was a special project. We were tracking the efficacy of a health supplement, something that was supposed to combat hair loss. I went through every single file."

That revelation opened up another bait bucket. Who made policy decisions, like the importance of conducting a hair loss study? I'd only seen Dr. Crecy a couple of times in the pharmacy, but he didn't strike me as a big-idea person. He seemed to be focused on his narrow dispensing tasks like Kasci, next door, was focused on baking pastries. (I had to call the guy Kasci, his new name, Stan, just wouldn't stick.)

And who conducted physical examinations at the Enclave to determine hair loss was a significant problem in the first place? Dr. Crecy didn't seem especially busy at the pharmacy, but I doubted he could be solely responsible for monitoring a thousand people. I'd done a rough count of the Enclave residences from the belfry, and guessed at the total number of tiny living units. One thousand was a conservative number, but a pretty high active case load for any single physician/pharmacist/Svengali.

The Enclave was certainly well-suited for medical experiments because it was self-contained. But who was observing and recording the results? You'd think an army of technicians with clipboards would be prowling the Enclave, asking questions and jotting down notes. And, anyway, you didn't need a giant wall or complex electronic brainwashing to study things like hair loss.

"What did you find out when you looked in Dr. Crecy's file?"

"He's had his prostate, testicles and seminal vesicles removed. Cancer. His dick is no longer a functional piece of machinery." Krystal shrugged. "Basically, I stopped worrying. Any lecherous behavior was just a pathetic form of compensation, like a little dog that keeps trying to hump things long after he's been fixed."

I experienced an instant of panic because my own sex drive seemed to be parked underneath a Walnut tree. I still had testicles and the occasional erection, but it was impossible to tell if a car was actually road worthy until you took it for a test drive. It's funny I employed that metaphor.

"Do you remember looking through *my* file?" I wondered if the fog was intended to keep people docile by dampening their sex drive. I wondered if the brain injury that sent me to the Enclave in the first place had impacted my libido.

"Oh, that project happened long before you came here." Krystal averted her eyes and looked slightly embarrassed, perhaps realizing I was pumping her for medical information about my own dick and seminal vesicles.

I really didn't want to be a little neutered dog, prompted by memory scraps to hump things while onlookers snickered.

There was an awkward pause in the conversation, and with the sudden silence, we both noticed an insect-like hum. The noise was quite near our tower, and deep memory suggested it was a colony of bees looking for a hive site. I worried they might inspect the interior of the metal bell and choose it for their new home. Krystal heard the noise too, she got to her feet and started to look around the belfry.

All aspects of nature deserve respect, but I didn't want to share my safe space with thousands of stinging roommates.

The noise increased and, suddenly, a small mechanical drone appeared, hovering at eye level, just beyond the western opening in the bell tower.

"Geez," Krystal said. "Someone's spying on us."

The machine continued to hover, making minute adjustments in position as if gauging the appropriate instant for an attack. I looked around the tower, but there was nothing I could use as a weapon, the scraps of lattice were too flimsy. I whispered: "have you ever seen drones here before?" I held my mouth in a rigid line in case the machine could lip-read.

"I've seen clouds of them fly over the Enclave. I always assumed they were from the military base, practicing maneuvers. I've never seen one up close before."

The drone was extremely wasplike in appearance. Directional cameras looked like bulbous eyes and there was some sort of proboscis that might have been a weapon or a sensor. A pair of long jointed legs hung underneath the body. It was difficult to see the lift mechanism because it was just a halo of movement. Presumably, rotors were spinning, but the action wasn't quite circular, rather the ellipsis of rapid wing movements.

Krystal picked up my sleeping bag from the floor and slowly twisted it into a long puffy rope. Then she leaned her upper body over the edge of the parapet. The drone moved slightly closer, as if in response. Krystal raised her right arm and snapped the sleeping bag like a whip.

I'm positive she missed the drone by several feet, but the machine exploded into tiny particles, never-the-less.

The mechanical noise continued, but it was now significantly different in tone. The wasp-like drone was instantly transformed into a cloud of tiny gnats and they all invaded the bell tower. I saw Krystal twisting her body and waving her arms as the mini robots flew into her nostrils and ears. I was rubbing them out of my eyes and trying to spit them from under my tongue.

I was terrified I was being stung, even though I couldn't feel any penetration from the microscopic stingers.

Krystal and I twirled around in the bell tower for several minutes, then the cloud of mechanical bugs retreated. I felt them vacate the beard stubble underneath my chin, and crawl from the hairline at the back of my neck. The tiny creatures re-massed outside the tower, well beyond sleeping-bag-whip range. We kept rubbing our skin and hair, feeling residual, psychological itchiness. We watched the floating-bug cloud darken and shrink.

The original drone was re-forming.

That was quite amazing because each individual insect must have had some sort of twirling mechanism that allowed it to fly. How did thousands of moving parts coalesce without shattering? It was impossible to say exactly when the cloud of individual bugs turned back into a single insect-machine. The rotor wings seemed to reform first, and the body and sensors that hung from it, last. But the whole process was quick enough to appear magical.

When the mass was once again a drone, it slowly circled the bell tower. We turned as well, facing it, bracing for what might happen next.

The ending was a little anticlimactic.

The drone lifted higher into the sky and the motor noise almost instantly disappeared. Krystal leaned over the parapet trying to track its flight, but my vertigo kept me centred within the turret.

"I can't even tell which direction it went," Krystal said.

We slumped into a sitting position, side by side against one of the parapet walls. The bell above our heads made echoey, resonant sounds as if the building was breathing.

Our conversation for the remainder of that day was pretty odd, because we generally avoided talking about the drone. You'd think our recent experience with a magic wall would prepare us for other unusual encounters, but that wasn't the case. The drone was such a surprise it was difficult to process. My brain struggled to integrate the exploding insect-machine into earlier paranoid theories.

Was the Enclave a military, rather than a medical experiment?

I closed my eyes and imagined all of my personality fragments sitting around a table in my brain's breakroom, discussing the mystery while they shuffled their feet and sipped coffee.

"Obviously, it wasn't a magic wall," one of the reasonable fragments of my brain declared. "Ripke just experienced another spontaneous nap, only this time he was standing up. Krystal saw his eyes drop like window blinds and she led his shuffling husk, back towards the community garden." The other personality fragments nodded around their coffee cups. "She can't be trusted," one of the paranoid slivers said.

I snapped out of it when Krystal asked me if I knew how to use a sextant.

That was a strange question and, of course, I didn't.

Krystal explained the Enclave's library currently had a display of old seafaring instruments. Could we take the sextant from a glass display case and use it to figure out our latitude, to find out where the community was really located?

I agreed that, theoretically, it was possible, if the instrument wasn't damaged…and if we could find an instruction manual, and if a cloud of insect drones didn't interfere. But that still wouldn't give the coordinates for longitude. We would only have half of the answer.

Krystal said we could calculate longitude based on the exact time lag between the Perseid meteor shower's appearance, and the predicted times for best viewing listed in the NYT newspaper article.

I didn't immediately see the value in calculating our exact position, but I was happy to see Krystal was showing some intellectual initiative. Maybe all it took was a slight reduction in mist exposure. She had spent a night on her roof watching meteors and a night with me in the steeple tower, and her attitude had shifted, significantly. "It's a lovely wall" had evolved into "let's steal a sextant to figure out our latitude."

I wanted to talk more about the wall, but I wanted to do it in a way that wouldn't make Krystal turn purple. I was still a little worried a weaponized implant was monitoring her speech, ready to explode at the first inappropriate word. "Is this the only walled enclave, or are there others? The newssheet said the founders wanted to create a template for future health care."

"I think this is the only one." Krystal's right index finger made little vibrations as if she were pushing invisible memory-buttons. "When I was recruited, there was no mention of alternate sites. It was just Ttupak."

Recruited.

"Do you think the wall is purely symbolic?" I asked, "a separation from the rest of the world, to help the patients heal?"

Krystal's face briefly darkened, then cleared. "No. Symbols don't need to be that high."

"I suppose you're right. There must be some purely practical reason for the wall, or no one would go to so much trouble constructing it."

"Right." She nodded. I examined her face. No colour change, no throbbing veins, a skull explosion no longer seemed imminent and I relaxed, slightly.

"Is the wall protecting us from some danger outside?"

Krystal laughed. "I doubt it, walls haven't been effective deterrents for two thousand years. Anyway, drones and helicopters can fly over our wall whenever they want. Our defenses aren't exactly impregnable."

"Is there something dangerous *inside* the Enclave that the walls are containing?"

Krystal shook her head. "No, of course not. It's not like a leper colony. I've seen the ambulance and helicopter crews, when they come from the outside. No one takes precautions, there's no Hazmat suits or decontamination procedure." She shrugged. "People here are really quite healthy, despite the average age. No one even gets colds. Last year, at the PharmaSave, we had to dispose of our cough syrup supply because it was so far past the expiry date. None of the residents ever needed the stuff. Basically, the pharmacy just sells make-up, toothpaste and moisturizer." She paused. "Maybe a few Band-aids."

"Reading glasses," I added.

"Yeah, a few." Krystal smiled.

To me, the purpose of the wall was obvious, but I wanted Krystal to say it. I didn't want to blurt out something that might be an expression of my head injury or paranoia and influence her. I wanted the information to be objectively real. That meant the words had to come from another mouth. "Well, what *is* the purpose of the wall?"

Krystal paused a moment before speaking, as if tasting the importance of her words. "The wall has to contain the fog."

"Thank you." I breathed a sigh of relief.

Wall and fog had to be interconnected. The Enclave was like a giant petri dish; it might not have a lid, but the walls were high enough to contain a heavy gaseous ingredient.

We had seen the fog penetrate tiny gaps in residential brickwork and windows, but the "wall" was a tougher obstacle. Up close, the slimy coating and joint sealant made it look impervious like molten glass.

If the petri dish metaphor was accurate, then the Enclave's inhabitants were the bacteria culture grown within its confines. The fog might be a nutrient, like agar, or some sort of inhibitor, or even a poison.

But why would anyone deliberately cultivate a bowl full of lazy, elderly people?

My paranoia fractalized. Maybe this group of pre-damaged residents had been collected precisely *because* they were expendable. Maybe we were being gassed and manipulated like monkeys and rats used to be, in ancient experiments.

"That's why you invited me to the bell tower," Krystal said, "to see the fog."

"Yes. I can't trust myself. I might have seen ordinary river mist and just imagined giant fans were blowing it through the community. If you hadn't walked with me, yesterday (I hoped it was only yesterday) I might have imagined I successfully circumvented the wall."

"Like Magellan."

"Yeah." The comparison was strangely relevant because Magellan got stalled less than halfway through his ancient sea journey around the world when a Mactan islander shot him in the nuts with a poison arrow. Anyway, if Krystal hadn't been with me, I probably would have invented a memory of crossing and re-crossing the river. "And I might have thought that exploding drone was just a dream, too," I added.

"Yes."

Of course, I was well aware of the potential paradox. If I was severely brain damaged, I might be hallucinating Krystal's very existence. But there wasn't any point in being incapacitated by skepticism, having faith in a shared reality was one of the necessities of life. When people rolled out of bed in the morning, they had to believe in basic things like floors and slippers and coffee.

I would continue to believe in Krystal until I woke up strapped to a gurney with a tongue-protector jammed in my mouth.

"But what's the purpose of the fog?" I asked. "I don't mean the immediate effect, where everyone is sleepy and conditioned to accept daily name changes. What's the end game? Are we being turned into compliant drones who will crawl into bombed-out buildings and shoot wounded enemies or abandoned babies?" I had been asleep for most of this war, so I didn't have a clear idea of what atrocities were going on.

Krystal chewed at the inside of her cheek. "That doesn't seem likely, does it? I mean, look at the demographic here. I can't imagine Rachel and Sigismund as urban guerillas. Now, if the military has adopted a strategy of sitting in lawn chairs and staring at a river until it capitulates, then we have an awesome secret weapon, here."

The sarcasm was a welcome new wrinkle in Krystal's character.

"Maybe they haven't completely worked out the bugs," I said. "They've figured out how to make people compliant, but haven't been able to combine that with energy, or initiative."

In a way, speculation was ridiculous because we didn't possess enough data. But it was better than wondering what your new name would be when you woke up.

"If the Enclave is a giant experiment, the controls are pretty loose," Krystal said. She probably felt a proper petri dish required a lid.

I nodded. "But we were just remotely violated by a drone; someone's observing us."

"Yeah."

I sensed the sky was darkening. I got up, shook the stiffness from my limbs and carefully leaned out through one of the belfry openings. I probably expected to see masses of birds again, but that wasn't the case. The sky was empty except for a dark purple cloud rolling over us.

"It's going to rain," I said.

Krystal smiled. "That's good."

"Why?"

"There'll be no fog, tonight. The mist would be dispersed in a downpour."

"Well, in that case, would you be willing to take another walk tonight, in the rain?"

"Sure." Krystal reached behind her and pulled out a small overnight bag she had been using as a back rest. She unzipped it, pulled out a clear, filmy bundle and passed it to me.

I unfolded a raincoat. "You'll need to wear this," I said, trying to return it.

Krystal immediately pulled out a second plastic poncho. "We did another product purge at the PharmaSave, today," she said. "Apparently, we don't sell a lot of raincoats."

"Okay."

The animals knew there wouldn't be fog tonight. The squirrels, raccoons and birds were all hunkered down close to the ground, anticipating a deluge. The weather was slightly cooler than yesterday, but still comfortable. I pulled on a sweater so I wouldn't feel chilled if we got soaked, later.

"Where are we going?"

"Back to that maintenance garage. It seems to be an access gate to the other side of the wall…"

I fell asleep mid-sentence.

"It's dark. C'mon, let's go." Krystal was shaking my shoulder.

I could hear heavy raindrops on the roof of the tower, and the metal bell seemed to be quietly echoing the noises. There was very little wind because the platform inside was still perfectly dry. I glanced at the distant turbines, and their blades were stationary.

I pulled the raincoat over my sweater, stood up and stretched. For the first time, I noticed Krystal and I were wearing the same type of shoes. Blond leather, with laces threaded through the heel, and textured rubber soles. In different circumstances, I would have called them "boat" shoes. They were perfect for clambering around in the rain.

Krystal was happy to move out, she almost slid down the ladder rails. As my feet touched the lawn, I lowered the ladder. "We're going to need this," I said. "We'll climb onto the roof of the garage and take a peek through the skylight. Then, if the coast is clear, we'll break in." I grabbed a brick from the pile of construction debris near the church doors.

I shouldered the ladder and started walking towards the communal garden, intending to retrace our earlier route, following the wall.

"That's not necessary," Krystal said. She tugged my arm like a leash, and we walked in the opposite direction. "The garage should be at the end of this road." We turned down Zelkova Street.

We were the only ones out walking, and after a few minutes we left houses behind entirely and were in a sort of park with hundreds of young trees, all of a uniform height. Far in front of us, we could see a bright yellow column extend from the maintenance garage skylight, like a beacon.

Someone was inside the building, working.

As we got closer, we started to jog, worried the person would suddenly exit and see us. I leaned the ladder against roof eaves and dropped the church brick onto the grass. We couldn't smash the skylight or door handles if the building was occupied. Raindrops sounded like miniature hammer blows on the metal sheathing, perfect for disguising our movements. Krystal climbed up first and stepped lightly onto the roof. She looked down at me and smiled. I guess there was no creaking or bowing.

The slick metal roof could have been treacherous, but there were hundreds of screwheads set into thick rubber washers protruding from corrugated ridges. The screws were perfect hand and toeholds. I felt more secure stepping onto that steep roof than I did climbing up and down the ladder in the bell tower.

Krystal and I migrated to different sides of the skylight and peeked over the edge. Most of the interior space was filled with vehicles. There was an ambulance, a passenger van, and a tractor with a front-end loader shovel. That was logical. There must be times when motorized machinery was useful, even in a lazy community like this. Each vehicle was tethered to a charging station by heavy cables.

The rear of the garage, the end that butted against the exterior wall, had a large roll-up steel door. **That door must open onto the mysterious space I could only think of as 'non-enclave.'**

Immediately below us, there was a large metal table. A man in a white lab coat was bent over the surface, working with a glinting metal tool.

He was probing the hairline of a naked male body.

I glanced over at Krystal, to gauge her reaction, but she was pointing violently at the skylight, insisting I pay attention. I looked through the glass again and saw the man in the lab coat remove a strip of skin from the neck with a probe, then hold it up towards the skylight.

We flinched, but he couldn't have seen us because he was wearing mini binoculars. They probably helped with his neck dissection, but more distant objects, like our faces, would have been a blur. It was hard to imagine why he contorted his upper body to display the patch of skin in that way. Maybe he was trying to better illuminate the sample with one of the powerful arc lights aimed at the table from different directions.

A large portion of the vivisectionist's face was hidden by those protruding goggles but I easily recognized him from his awkward smile. His white lips formed a rigid rectangle, revealing slightly crooked teeth. I had seen him in the parkette earlier, sweeping the street, and cutting grass with a primitive push lawn-mower. He had waved and smiled at me then, and I was reminded of the gasping mouth of a dying perch.

The white lab coat covered an orange jumpsuit. The lawn maintenance man was moonlighting as a coroner. I wondered if Dr. Crecy knew he had competition.

The maintenance man plopped his skin sample into a biopsy jar.

There was very little blood on the incision-site, so I assumed the person was dead.

The maintenance man grabbed the body by the shoulders and roughly rolled him over onto his back.

I could now recognize the patient/victim. It was Kasci or Tyler or Stan, the man who ran the little bakery beside the PharmaSave. His eyes were opened wide and unblinking. The lawn maintenance-man/physician placed the biopsy jar in a large fridge then lumbered back, carrying a wicker basket full of oysters.

Holy fuck, the man was going to snack on seafood while he worked.

I glanced at Krystal to see if she was registering the same horrible sight, and she nodded.

The maintenance man took another utensil from a tray. This tool looked like a miniature gelato scoop. He used the implement to pop out Kasci's eyeballs. He applied little clamps to the trailing optic nerves then snipped off the threads connecting the orbs to the brain. The man tossed the eyeballs into the wicker container.

The basket wasn't full of oysters, it was loaded to the brim with eyeballs.

Krystal looked ill.

The man returned his bucket of eyeballs to the fridge, then grabbed another instrument, and made a long incision in Kasci's right thigh. He stuck his fingers in the slit, worked them around and pulled out a surprisingly large silver cannister. The man clamped several nerve-like cords, much as he had with the eyeballs, then snipped the connections. The cannister went into a metal tray.

Kasci's left arm was flopped over his head and the man made a quick incision in his armpit and used a pair of forceps to remove a subcutaneous bit of black plastic smaller than my thumbnail. A thread was cut, and the bit of plastic was dropped into the metal tray beside the cannister. I thought I could hear a clink, but I must have been imagining it, because the rain battering the roof overpowered all other noise.

The lawn maintenance man made another incision in Kasci's right armpit, then his throat, then his groin. More bits of plastic were removed and dropped into the metal tray. The work was done very quickly, like you might prune a rose bush if you had years of practice.

A sudden loud, mechanical sound came from within the garage and our view was obscured by a moving metal panel. Both the sound and movement were shocking, because we were so intently focused on the dissection. The rear garage door had slid up on its tracks, but I couldn't have been more surprised if a whale had swum through my field of vision.

Krystal reached across the skylight to slap my shoulder, then she slid down the metal roof incline, her shoes making squeaky *itch itch itch* sounds on the raised screwheads. I followed at a much slower pace.

We didn't know if the interlopers intended to take Kasci's corpse through the wall, or if they would open the front garage door and enter the Enclave. Krystal pulled the ladder off the eaves and grabbed the top rails before it clattered to the ground. I picked up the feet and we ran along the base of the wall until its shadow fully absorbed us.

We crouched beside each other to watch the garage. The skylight only emitted scraps of yellow, now, which meant the sliding perimeter-wall door was still open. When a thick column of light cut the darkness like a scalpel, we figured the door was back in its closed position and the visitors had returned to their outside world.

Then the light disappeared altogether, and I felt the panic of utter blindness, because there was no ambient light from Enclave buildings, and the moon was obliterated by clouds. Because there was no vehicle traffic in the community, there were no streetlights to illuminate the roads. No one was up late reading.

The front garage door slid up and we saw a blob separate from the black mass of the building and move down Zelkova Street.

"It's the maintenance man," Krystal said. "He's pushing his cart."

"How come you don't know his name?" I asked.

There was a long pause. "That's...I don't know. I guess he's never come into the PharmaSave. I've never thought to ask his name."

I wondered why that particular name wasn't part of Krystal's latest data infusion.

We waited for more than an hour, huddled against the base of the wall, wondering if the maintenance man was going to return; with another corpse.

Waiting was pleasant enough because our bodies were pressed together, as if we were trying to relearn what simple human contact was like.

Of course, there was no amount of time that made Zelkova Street a safe passage, so we took the long way back, following the wall to the community garden. I let my left-hand fingers brush against the textured concrete surface, daring the structure to twist like a snake and send us in a different direction.

We stopped by the church just long enough to return the neighbour's ladder, and then walked to my apartment on Walnut Street.

I opened the door with my ID card and turned on a small electric heater. Krystal tied a clothesline to two eyelets fixed in the walls. I wasn't aware our units had a system to hang wet clothing.

Krystal stripped, facing away from me, then wrung her clothes out in a small sink. She climbed onto the unpadded kitchen chair, her body a silhouette in my apartment's only window, and hung her clothes on the line above the heater. When she was done, she climbed down, turned around and rubbed her hair. Her fingernails were now metallic green, the bits of colour playing hide-n-seek in the wet curls. I couldn't remember her applying the polish: it might have been done at the PharmaSave while I was sleeping underneath a giant metal church bell. "I'm going to take a shower,"

Krystal said and padded into the bathroom.

I stared at the muscles in her lower back, watched them flex and relax with each footfall. I took off my clothes, squeezed out as much water as I could and hung them on the line as well. I moved the doormat underneath to catch any drips.

Then I stood in the doorway of the tiny bathroom and watched pinkish blobs of skin form abstract patterns in the condensation of the tiny shower tube.

After what felt like a year or two, the door opened an inch and a pink steam-finger extended and curled, inviting me in.

5

"First things first," Krystal said, the next morning. "We have to get a pastry."

I knew what she meant, we had to see if Kasci was in the bakery or not. If he greeted us with a smile and suggested the "usual," we would have to re-think everything we had seen in the maintenance garage last night. Essentially, we would have to face the fact craziness is contagious and I'd infected Krystal.

It was a stressful walk, made slightly easier because we held hands for several blocks. Krystal let go as we approached the little business district and began encountering people walking towards the river parkette.

"Hello Rachel," Krystal said to the elderly lady I'd previously encountered. She was still wearing a brightly coloured sun dress, but with a different pattern. "Hello Sigismund." The same little bulldog followed the lady, trailing his leash. The animal looked up when he heard his name, and smiled the way bulldogs smile.

I was relieved last night's rain had prevented another wholesale identity shift.

We looked both ways, then skipped across Alder Street and went in the bakery doors.

My heart sank because Kasci was sprinkling icing sugar on a tray of jelly doughnuts. When he heard the door open, he turned around to face us and he wasn't Kasci anymore, he was another baker, with similar dark hair and a similar physique.

"Hello, Orest," Krystal greeted him. I'm not sure when she realized we were dealing with a replacement, but the proper new name popped out of her mouth, right on cue.

"Hi there, Krystal, hey Carol." The new guy knew the names currently printed on our ID cards. "The usual?"

"Sure."

This time, it was café au lait with a banana cream doughnut for me, and a black coffee with a raspberry Danish for Krystal.

"Hey Orest," I said, "did you ever hear the story about how I got my nickname?" I was curious about the depth of the data transfer. Kasci had quickly dredged up the story of a supposed childhood brush-cut that looked like a block of cheese. Apparently, my little friends teased me about it by calling me "Cheddar-head," and when that seemed like too much work, shortened it to "Ched."

"A haircut, wasn't it?" The baker frowned. "I can't remember who told me that."

"Hey," Krystal asked, "when did you ship in?"

"Just a few days ago." The response was quick. "I was on a waiting list for more than two years, though. I thought I was going to be deployed to Ceylon, so I was really happy when a spot opened up in the Enclave." He nodded several times.

We saluted with our coffees and left the store.

"I've got to work for a couple of hours," Krystal said. "I can pick up our supplies at the end of my shift." She looked around to make sure the seniors in the parkette were busy watching the brown water, then she kissed me on the cheek and wandered into the PharmaSave. I checked for traffic and crossed over to the parkette.

I wondered what "supplies" she was referring to.

The very old man, who I'd seen fishing for perch, was walking along the water's edge. The man I assumed was his son walked beside him, keeping a firm grip on his forearm. Two ladies passed them and there was an exchange of "good day," "nice day" "such a nice boy."

A few minutes later, I heard one of the ladies say, "Oh yes, it's a lovely wall, we've got no complaints there." I sat down in an aluminum lawn chair in front of a Maple tree that seemed poised to jump off the bank and into the water. I felt uneasy, like I was walking in a circle, yet had somehow lost my way.

Of course, I fell asleep. This time, I finished my doughnut and café au lait first. When I woke, the empty cup and napkin were in the grass at my feet.

The sun was very high in the sky, and my mouth felt dry.

Krystal and I had made some sort of a plan, I remembered that much. But what was it? I got up and walked towards the garbage can near the parking platform, so I could throw away my coffee cup.

A man in orange coveralls was pushing a large, wheeled cart

in the same direction. I suppose he was about to empty the parking lot garbage into the hopper attached to the front of his cart. Looking at his back, I couldn't tell if this was the same man who had gouged out Kasci's eyes like melon balls. I waited until he was almost at the garbage can, then I called out: "Hey!"

He turned to face me and his white lips formed a rectangle that was supposed to be a smile. He looked like a fish that had just been pulled into a parallel universe.

If the man recognized me as one of the spies who had watched him through a rainy skylight, he gave no indication. He raised his right hand in a wave, and I saw Krystal's face appear underneath his elbow. She had been hunched inside the garbage can and rose to her feet after the man turned to greet me.

I remembered.

We had planned to kidnap the maintenance worker; we had discussed it for hours last night. But my brain had slipped a pulley and I almost napped through my part.

Krystal reached around the man's face and pressed a damp napkin over his mouth. His eyes briefly became fisheyes, then he collapsed. I jogged forwards and caught him in my arms before he clattered into his cart.

I ducked down, stuck my shoulder into his stomach and lifted him into the air, like a sleepy toddler. Krystal leapt out of the garbage can, elevated the man's feet and guided them into the garbage hopper on his cart. I lowered the rest of his body and he filled the container like banana cream fills a doughnut.

Krystal wound several loops of tape around the man's head, fixing the damp napkin over his nose.

KANTZ.

I remembered now, that was the product Krystal used to disable the man. It was marketed as ant spray, but the label indicated the chemical inside was 99% chloroform. So, it could have been sold in PharmaSave's kidnapping aisle as well as its household pest section.

"I was wondering if you were going to show up," Krystal said.

"I fell asleep." My voice must have sounded incredibly sad, because she didn't criticize the incompetence. Krystal squeezed my upper arm.

"I woke you up just before I moved into position." She looked into my eye holes. "I should have made sure you were ready." Krystal looked around as she spoke. Several elderly ladies were approaching, but they didn't act like they'd just witnessed an assault.

"Good day, Hilda," Krystal smiled, "good day, Veronica."

"Krystal, Carol." I don't think I'd ever seen these people before, yet they still knew me.

We checked for traffic and pushed the wheeled cart across the street. Then we walked by the alphabetized forest: Catalpa, Dogwood, Elm…

No one seemed to care the wrong people were pushing the maintenance cart.

"Hey Raymond," Krystal said to the person who shared nine Walnut Street with me.

Walnut, Xylopia, Yew…

We turned down Zelkova and were almost at the maintenance garage when Krystal paused and rooted around in the garbage hopper. She emerged, smiling, holding the maintenance man's ID card.

"Now, we don't have to break in." Krystal held the card close to her nose. "Beverly Beckford," she read. "Grey eyes, no home address."

"Maybe he lives outside of the Enclave," I suggested and squeezed in to have a closer look at the card. It had a stamp on the back, sort of like Krystal's. I wondered if the marking delineated people who were on "staff" at the Enclave, distinguishing them from people like me who had no function besides the consumption of pastry.

The garage seemed to have grown after last night's rain. In my memory, it wasn't much more than a shed but, in fact, it was a substantial building with three over-sized garage doors facing the Enclave. There was also a man-door, with a card reader, very similar to the one outside my apartment on Walnut Street.

Krystal inserted Beverly's card, opened the main door, then went inside. A moment later, one of the large doors rolled up and I was able to wheel the cart inside. Krystal pushed a button and the door closed again. The skylight didn't provide much illumination because the structure was now in the shadow of the wall. But there were powerful spotlights on rolling platforms. Krystal turned one on, and the garage was brightly, almost painfully lit.

"Let's get Beverly out of the garbage hopper." We had to tip the pail onto the floor, then slide the maintenance man out. I managed to hoist him onto the metal table where he had dissected Kasci.

"Here." Krystal found some plastic zip ties on a work bench, the kind of thing a gardener might use to secure young tomato plants to wooden stakes. We used a dozen strips to bundle his hands and feet. Then Krystal removed the soggy napkin from his face.

"When do you think he'll wake up?"

"I don't know. I'm surprised he went down so easily; I barely touched the paper to his face." She pressed two fingers into Beverly's neck. "His pulse is really weak. I feel *something* though."

I bent over the man's face and heard a faint whistling in his nose. "He's breathing." I looked at the garage door that separated the Enclave from the outside world, and wished it had a window. I wanted to raise the panel, but fear trumps curiosity. "Let's take a look around the garage."

Peering through the skylight last night, the building seemed crammed with vehicles. Now that we were inside, we could see additional space for storage lockers ringing the building.

Krystal pulled one of those doors open.

It was like an over-sized closet, full of shirts, dresses and jackets on hangers. Shoes, hats, pants, socks and underwear were neatly stacked on shelves. The clothing looked like the discarded husks of human beings, and it affected me more deeply than I could have imagined.

I opened the door of the large refrigerator I had noticed last night. There was a blast of cold air and a whiff of ozone. Dozens of biopsy jars were stacked on shelves, like ancient condiment bottles. I pulled a few out to inspect the contents: hair, fingernails, teeth, patches of skin.

The wicker basket was on a chest-high shelf. It was heavy and I let it thump on the ground at my feet. Sure enough, it was full of eyeballs, trailing their optic nerves. There must have been dozens, perhaps hundreds, and they were squished together like a pail full of winter dog shit.

I guess you could say it was wasteful and disrespectful to keep a collection of eyes in a wicker basket but, primarily, I was struck with the oddness of it.

"Here's a map." Krystal pointed to an aerial drawing of the Enclave mounted on a bare patch of wall. Every single building seemed to be included, I could even recognize the accurate positioning of individual trees in the parkette. There were no buildings marked outside the Enclave walls, but two vertical lines at the top and bottom margins, suggested an extended barrier. Maybe the Enclave was a salient in a truly massive structure.

Of course, maps are only as trustworthy as their cartographers.

"No bridges across the river," I said. At least that detail matched my own partial observations.

"No bridges," Krystal echoed.

The crop on the opposite side of the river was labeled "tobacco," and there was a circular landing pad marked out, near the wind turbines. I guess I was wrong about the crop being soy plants, and I was wrong about a bridge being absolutely necessary to maintain them. The tobacco harvest must be accomplished with the help of a helicopter. A network of purple lines originated at the wind turbines and crossed the river. I supposed they marked underground conduits collecting hydro power. The library seemed to be a central distribution hub, radiating more purple lines to the residential streets.

Blue lines in the river must indicate fog pipes. They seemed to terminate in the volunteer fire station.

Krystal pulled open a wooden drawer full of file folders.

A vestigial memory clicked into my mental slide carousel, and I realized how ridiculous and primitive it was to have paper records. Krystal thumbed through the label tabs, then pulled one file from the mass and read a few paragraphs.

"The tobacco plants are a 'surrogate,' producing an organic vaccine." She looked at me and smiled. "That seems very clever."

I don't know why she chose to investigate that particular bit of our mystery. Maybe the situation was so bizarre, it wasn't yet possible to process the entirety. We had to focus on trivialities like the crop growing on the opposite riverbank. Once again, I thought of the two elderly ladies saying "it's a lovely wall." The brain copes by parsing the world into manageable bits.

We heard Beverly groaning on the metal table and turned to

face him.

He squinted back at us. "Why did you do that?" he asked, genuinely puzzled. He rubbed his mouth with his thumbs, as if the ant spray left an unpleasant taste on his lips. At the same time, he noticed that his wrists were zip-tied together. "Why have you tied me up?"

"Tell us what's going on, here." I tried make my voice sound threatening, but my heart suddenly wasn't in it. There was something disabling about Beverly's reaction to being kidnapped. He was mildly *annoyed* rather than terrified.

"You didn't have to take me out," he said, "you could have just asked me, like last time."

"Last time?" I nervously scratched a patch of skin underneath my throat.

"Ah…" Beverly snorted. "I knew you wouldn't remember."

Krystal grabbed a tool off a workbench and waved it in Beverly's face. "Never mind the bullshit." She was much more menacing. The tool looked like an awl or an ice pick. I had seen it lying in the tray during Kasci's dissection.

Beverly rolled his eyes. "Okay, we'll play twenty questions again. But first, let me ask *you* a couple of things."

Krystal and I made wary eye contact.

"When's the last time either of you went to the bathroom?" He waited, but we didn't respond. I hadn't gone to the bathroom in days, unless I'd taken care of business while sleepwalking. I glanced at Krystal and her face looked like a wall. "And what have you eaten in the last couple of days?" Beverly asked. "A Danish or two? Some coffee? Doesn't that strike you as odd?"

It's difficult to describe how those simple questions staggered me, even as I recognized the unpleasant truth lurking within them. Krystal and I looked at our shoes.

Beverly sighed. "You know, it will probably save us some time if you let me handle the F.A.Q." He didn't wait for a response. "You don't *need* to eat, you only do it out of habit. Some of the material is metabolized as fuel, the remainder is respirated. No excretion necessary." He held up a finger as if he intended to count off a number of points. But the plastic zip-ties made that gesture awkward, so he gave up.

Krystal took the opportunity to intrude. "The drone…"

"I use a modified Vespula as a medical monitor. It would be impossible for me to treat eleven hundred patients without a robot assistant."

"Dr. Crecy."

"My *human* assistant. He's useless."

"The eyeballs…" Krystal's voice was anguished.

"I'm not a sadist, I have to excise eyeballs to verify the fog still eliminates eye-lice."

"Eye lice?" I felt as stupid as any echo.

"Yes. They're indicators of catastrophic decay." Beverly pursed his lips and pretended to think. "What else would you like to know, what else…" He wanted to regain control of the conversation. "You're probably still curious about what's on the other side of the wall. Well, it's still only ten thousand greenhouses. You weren't impressed when I showed them to you last time, and it hasn't changed since. *That's* the animate future, not some Asian battle-field. If you weren't lounging here in the Enclave, you'd be spend-ing your days picking aphids off heritage tomato plants and crush-ing the bugs with your fingernails."

In a way, I admired Beverly. He had been incapacitated with ant spray, trussed with plastic zip-ties and threatened with a sharp-ened screwdriver. Yet he was still able to adopt the mildly sarcastic tone of a middle-school teacher, berating a pair of disobedient students. He continued the lesson. "Your name changes and memory enhancements are intended to…"

"Enhancements?" Krystal spat the word.

"Yes, enhancements. They are part of a remarkable training protocol: basic skills are retained but each day has the excitement of a fresh beginning."

"You can't be serious." Krystal rolled the tool in her fingers.

The pink tip of Beverly's tongue poked out, then withdrew. It was the first miniscule sign of stress. He was afraid of Krystal. "I'll never diminish your feelings," he said, "but, ultimately, you *agreed* to this, we *all* agreed…"

"I didn't consent to be some sort of lab rat," Krystal said.

"I don't want to quibble, I know this situation is difficult to comprehend, but the 'consent' really was vetted by the Supreme Court…"

"Bullshit. I didn't consent to be a lab rat." Krystal's lips turned white.

Beverly closed his eyes as if he were suddenly very tired. "No, you didn't. That would be illogical as well as impossible because lab rats are still alive."

There was a long pause. I was desperately trying to remember the last time I'd bitten a fingernail or shaved. I'd only been awake for a few days but some bodily changes should have been noticeable even over that brief period of time. I sighed. Lab rats regularly shed fur and went to the bathroom in clumps of wood shavings, and that suddenly seemed unfair. I pointed a finger at Beverly. "I want to make sure I understand what you're saying. You seem to be implying..." It was difficult to put into words "...that we..." I waved the finger between my chest and Krystal "...are *not* alive."

"According to the Dredrick Skott ruling, you're not." Some air whistled in Beverly's nose.

"We're not dead," Krystal said, and I felt deeply sorry for her, having to justify the most self-evident of all propositions. "Dead people can't...have sex."

"Oh, no?" Beverly giggled as if he had made a joke, but his expression quickly moderated. "You're absolutely right, you're not 'dead.' The voguish term is *animate*." His pupils rolled upwards. "Think about how difficult it has been, historically, to define terms like 'life' and 'death,' and how unreliable each definition has been: the presence or absence of respiration, of a pulse or certain neurological sparks..."

"Bullshit." Krystal's lips were just inches from Beverly's nose.

I pushed between them and Krystal retreated a step. "What's the point of this community?" I asked. "We aren't producing anything in the Enclave, we aren't *doing* anything. What's the point?"

"Failure."

"What?"

"The determination of an absolute." Beverly's lips formed a white rectangle, his personal version of a smile. "They used to say the human body completely regenerates itself every seven years, but that's simply not true. Neurons are never replaced, while skin cells and stomach cells and blood cells are created almost daily." Eyes flicked back and forth between us. "*That's* the point of the Enclave. You're allowed to take your little walks and play in the garden and fish while we determine exactly how long a human body can function after it loses the ability to generate new cells."

I scratched the stubble under my chin.

"Decimattu and Arakpak invented the procedure fifty years ago. If you fortify organs with pumps, insert a battery pack into the quadricep, and bathe the tissue every night in a medicinal fog …well…the old container holds up pretty well, even if there's no renewal."

"How long?" Krystal asked.

"Initially, it was only a few weeks, but thanks to the Enclave, we've been stretching it out." Beverly pointed at me with his bound hands. "You're a medical oddity, son, you've lasted longer than we could ever hope." He narrowed his eyes. "But I suspect we may be approaching the finish tape." His lips made a smacking noise as he clipped off the last word. "Taypah."

"We're walking corpses?" Bits of spittle flicked off Krystal's lips like liquid shrapnel. Our bodies must be programed to produce that effluent. I thought of the little subcutaneous chips that had been removed from Kasci's body. They must be sophisticated mini processors.

"You're not corpses," Beverly said, "you're *animate*." He averted his face. "I apologize, but I'm not the one who wrote the majority decision." His voice became louder, as if he were reading a proclamation. "A body that no longer generates new cells, yet artificially mimics life processes prior to catastrophic physical decay, shall be deemed *animate* and subject to the following protections…"

Krystal jammed the awl into Beverly's neck.

The man's eyes widened in surprise then he produced a series of sounds, like a tiny electric motor seizing: *eck eck eck*.

Krystal withdrew the tool and jammed two fingertips into the wound and wriggled them. She withdrew a plastic chip, similar to the ones removed from Kasci's body. The chip trailed a hair-like wire and Krystal yanked it free. I couldn't help touching my own throat; I felt a squarish bump under the flesh.

"We need this," Krystal said, "to operate the vehicles. It's some sort of biometric transponder." Clearly, she now remembered details from our previous encounter with Beverly. We must have taken a ride with him outside the Enclave but been persuaded to return.

I touched the little device in my throat again. Perhaps I was defective, because similar memories were not surfacing within me. But I did have the ability to process new information. For example, I knew our departure from the Enclave, this time, would be permanent.

"Take Beverly's ID card and open the wall door."

I followed Krystal's instructions. The metal panels clicked, and rolled up, and there was a certain amount of drama as the curtain raised.

When the world beyond the Enclave walls was revealed, I was disappointed.

We saw a broad unpaved road, a straight line of packed gravel, that turned into a thread, then into a dot as it neared a distant horizon. The road was flanked by opaque, glass-walled buildings, the greenhouses Beverly had mentioned.

That's the animate future, he had said. I wondered how many individuals were wandering through those glass corridors, picking kale, drinking coffee and avoiding the washrooms.

There was a puff of dust on the road, several miles away. A vehicle was approaching, although it was impossible to tell if it was speeding towards the Enclave in response to a mysterious distress signal, or if it intended to veer into the maze of glass buildings.

We watched the burgeoning cloud for a few seconds, and Krystal frowned. Some additional memories were troubling her. "I don't think we should leave this way."

What other way was there? There were no more doors in the wall. And there wasn't any grappling equipment hanging in the garage, that might enable us to climb over. Anyway, my vertigo would disable me if we found a system of hooks and ropes.

Should we attack the approaching driver with ant spray, like we ambushed Beverly?

No, that was far too risky. We didn't know how many people were in the vehicle. "Let's go to the river," I suggested.

Crystal pushed a button and the garage door slid down, hiding the greenhouses. We left by the Enclave door and closed it behind us. We jogged down Zelkova Street, past the alphabetized list of trees. "We can swim through the wall," I said, "one of those depressions where the wall crosses the river. They let the water through, so they'll let us through as well." Earlier, I had assumed those openings were sluiceways for a hydro generator, but there was no indication of any such system on the map we inspected. The passages seemed to be simple flow apertures.

Of course, the river water had to form a fog-proof seal against the concrete, so if we entered the tubes, we might be drowned rather than shredded by mechanical screws.

"Okay." Krystal didn't seem daunted by the risk. "Can you swim?"

"I don't know." It was a sad admission. I looked behind us, but no one was pursuing. If people in that vehicle intended to capture us, maybe they would waste time searching all the closets in the maintenance garage before charging through the Enclave.

We ran across Balsam Street to the parkette, without checking for traffic first.

"It's a lovely day," Rachel said to us. The hem of her sun dress flapped as we sped past.

"Hello Rachel, hello Sigismund," Krystal said, automatically.

I waded into the river. The water was shallow, but the muck grabbed at my shoes. I had to lay down and take a couple of splashy strokes away from shore. "I can swim," I said, over my shoulder. Krystal was suddenly beside me.

The black fog-nozzles seemed to turn towards us like snake heads.

A few people sitting in lawn chairs raised their noses, but no one pointed, or left their seats.

We worked our way to the floating buoy line and ducked underneath the connecting rope. I looked over my shoulder to make sure the fog pipes weren't swimming after us. The current was stronger here, but not frightening. People in the park continued reading or doing crossword puzzles. We floated towards a faded orange sign that said: DANGER KEEP AWAY. Metal grills angled from the wall, but they were designed to deflect large pieces of floating debris, and we easily squeezed between the bars. I hung on to the grill, and the current pulled my feet near the surface. I looked at Krystal, and she nodded at me. I took a deep breath, then released my grip and slipped into the algae-slick concrete tube.

I was only fully submerged for a few seconds, but terror

made it difficult to hold my breath for even that short period of time. I scraped through the brick passageway, then my stomach dipped as I slid down a hill sculpted from brown liquid. It wasn't an actual waterfall, thankfully, just a smooth decline between two distinct elevations. I bumped my hip on something at the bottom then, after a period of disorientation where I couldn't tell which way was up, my head popped to the surface all on its own, in a soapy cloud of froth.

"Ah!" I heard a voice and Krystal was beside me again, with wet hair plastered over her eyes and mouth. Her upper body quivered like a fishing bobber as she wrestled the hair back behind her ears. "Are you alright?" My poor swimming technique had probably alarmed her.

"Yes." My skin was tea-colored under the water. I waved my arms for stability as the current gently moved us downstream. We floated for a long time, then my toes scraped against a rift of gravel. I stood with my chin above the water and wiped the dirty foam from my face. The river was much narrower on this side of the wall, but the banks were higher, and crested with mounds of emerald grass. We worked our way to the edge, where the water was only knee-deep, but the muddy walls looked difficult to scale, so we kept sloshing downstream.

It was hard to imagine what sort of landscape would have greeted us had we managed to climb out of the river, but there were no overhanging trees or looming buildings. A single wasp-like drone flew overhead, and we momentarily panicked and ducked between the hanging grass and the mud bank. But the machine didn't appear to be hunting for us, it just sped towards the enclave, roughly following the river.

As we walked, the sun dried our shirts and the river became progressively shallower. At one point, it was split into two by the rocky hump of an island. We scrambled up to the top of that mass and saw a small wooden sign, painted with faded red letters: WELCOME. The font reminded me of the bait bucket I had seen during the first minutes of my new consciousness.

Krystal tousled her hair, letting a breeze infiltrate the curls. "It feels good to be alive," she said.

I didn't bother correcting her.

From the island crest, we had a decent view of the surrounding countryside. It seemed to be an empty rolling prairie, or per-haps an enormous estuary. There were lots of low hills, or dunes, so we couldn't see a firm horizon, the area seemed open and limitless. Perhaps that effect was just our minds reacting to the wall's sudden absence. Behind us, the Enclave still looked gigantic, even though the structure was now several miles away. I could, in fact, see bits of wall extending from the sides of the enclosure, as indicated on the map. It was impossible to tell how long those sections were because they were absorbed by the bumpy terrain. I had a feeling this part of the planet was divided by a tremendously long physical barrier.

The shadow of a drone flitted in front of us for a few sec-onds, its existence momentarily camouflaged in the dappled sur-face of the water. When we noticed it and looked upward, the device was just a disinterested speck moving towards the enclave.

We finally sloshed out of the river at the foot of a low wood-en bridge.

The bridge was part of a thoroughfare, roughly north-south, parallel to the enclave's extended walls. Six clunky bicycles were leaning against the rails of the bridge, their front wheels all point-ing in the same direction.

There was another painted sign, hanging next to the bicycles. The words simply said: USE ME.

So, we did.

ABOUT THE AUTHOR

Mark Thomas is a writer and artist living in St. Catharines, Canada. He is the author of several Sci Fi and mystery books, including **Next to Ewe, A Robot, a Ghost and an Alien walk into a Bar**, and. **Searching for Martian Slutfest IV**.

Check out his website <u>https://flamingdogshit.com</u>.

More Books from WolfSinger Publications

Blue Grass Dreams Aren't for Free — Gerri Leen

These racehorses can talk, race riderless, and manage their own careers thanks to genetic manipulation in the past intended to make Thoroughbreds hardier. But living free doesn't mean living without problems of the career and family (both blood and found) kind. Nor does it mean they are free from having to interact with humans.

In this mosaic novel, stories of two very different stallions and their friends and families (both four legged and two) interconnect to explore how these horses deal with career decisions, love, family, retirement, illness, and having to find alternate paths when flat racing does not prove a profitable or fulfilling life choice.

Not all roads lead to the winner's circle, and even when they do, winning doesn't always equal happiness without someone to share it with.

Midnight Menagerie — edited by Carol Hightshoe

Step right up, dear traveler—your ticket to the extraordinary awaits.

Beneath the striped canopies of the *Midnight Menagerie*, wonders stir and nightmares awaken. Strongmen flex their might, fortune tellers spin futures, and acrobats defy the stars. But if it is shadows you seek—if you are drawn to the hush of velvet-draped corners where the line between spectacle and sorcery blurs—then step closer.

Here, within these pages, beasts from beyond the veil prowl in cages not quite strong enough. Carnival performers barter in secrets instead of silver. Mystics weave illusions that refuse to fade, and every whispered promise carries a cost. From the neon glow of alien menageries to the flickering lantern light of haunted carnivals, *Midnight Menagerie* is a collection of the eerie, the wondrous, and the strange.

So take your seat, dear reader. The lights are dimming, the curtains are rising…and the show is about to begin.

The World of the Moho – Tyree Campbell

Aldon (Allie) McIntyre, a white American geologist with a thirst for adventure, and Thadie Mayane, a Black South African mining supervisor with a commanding presence, are exploring the depths of an abandoned mine when the floor collapses, hurling them into an extraordinary realm known as Below. Nestled between the Earth's crust and mantle, this vast world is home to breathtaking landscapes, intelligent species—some friendly, others predatory—and dangers unlike anything they've ever imagined.

Forced to rely on each other for survival, Allie and Thadie must navigate treacherous terrain, fend off alien predators, and face the looming threat of capture by those who see them as little more than slaves. As they search for the legendary passage back to Above, their uneasy alliance will be tested by the perilous environment—and the prejudices and mistrust they each carry.

Will they overcome the trials of Below and find their way back Above? Or will this stunning and dangerous world consume them entirely—if they don't destroy each other first?

Mars in Carnage – William Paul Lazarus

Humanity's dream of colonizing Mars quickly becomes a fight for survival. Mission director Lt Col. John Hathaway sends astronauts Aadya "Kate" Khatun and Hamza "Arti" Artsruni to explore and establish a foothold on the Red Planet. One astronaut is killed, during what appears to be an alien attack; the other makes a solo, dangerous return to a hero's welcome on Earth.

Over a century later a Martian colony has firmly established —the underground city of Katarti, Cecil Townley, a tour guide for visitors to Mars is captured by a band of terrorists trying to end what they believe are horrible governmental actions on Mars. Hiding in underground tunnels, they begin their attack with Townley forced to be their guide. Their actions introduce him to a world he never knew existed, far from the innocent tale he had been telling newcomers for years.

Cowboy Up – edited by Carol Hightshoe

Cowboy Up gathers stories that celebrate the timeless tradition of rodeo. The dust, the grit, the glory—it's all here.

From the echoes of the past to the rodeo arenas of today, these stories will take you on a wild ride through the highs and lows of rodeo life. You'll share in their triumphs and their heartbreaks. From the unbreakable bond between rider and horse to the courage it takes to get back in the saddle after a fall, this anthology is a tribute to the spirit that keeps rodeo alive.

But this book isn't just about telling stories. It's about giving back. Eighty-Five percent of proceeds from Cowboy Up will be donated to the Justin Cowboy Crisis Fund, a non-profit organization dedicated to helping injured rodeo athletes get back on their feet. Your purchase helps support those who risk it all in the arena, offering them a lifeline when they need it most.

So saddle up. Dive into these tales of resilience, heart, and the cowboy way. With every story, you're not just reading about rodeo —you're helping to keep its spirit alive.

Homefall Search – Dana Bell

Charged with finding the best place for a new Homefall, Jehna Talon searched on Saris, a world located in the Tashiti Nebula. Along with her Arial shapeshifter companions, she goes into the Ghost Mountains to find a specific valley, only to become trapped during a storm and encounters a native dragon.

With local rancher Harrison Talbot she negotiates the price for the land. Brides, for him and his hands. As her uncle taught her, there's always a need to be filled. Traveling to Aris and with the help of a local contact, she finds women willing to brave the frontiers of space.

Returning to Ronia, home of the Talons, she learns opposition from the other clan leaders may stop the dream she had of becoming a clan leader. They argue there are too few Rovers, and she'll never succeed.

Could they be right, despite her already finding the ideal location?

The Dragon's Hoard 3 – edited by Carol Hightshoe

In this anthology, twenty-six authors weave enchanting stories of dragons—from the fierce and fire-breathing to the wise and benevolent. Enter a treasure trove of tales where dragons reign supreme, and hoards are more than mere gold.

Discover hidden gems of wisdom and magic within these lairs. Feast on tales that shimmer with magic, adventure, and the timeless allure of dragons. Explore the myriad treasures dragons hold dear and the legends that surround them.

From heartwarming tales of friendship and loyalty to thrilling adventures filled with danger and magic, these tales offer something for every dragon lover. Whether they are guardians of treasure, seekers of knowledge, or forces of nature: the dragons in this collection will ignite your imagination.

The Dragon's Hoard 2 – edited by Carol Hightshoe

Welcome to realms where dragons reign, treasures abound, and every adventure leads to magic. Explore stories that spark the imagination and might just awaken the dragon within. Are you brave enough to face the dragon and claim your prize?

From the unyielding grip of ancient magics to the cunning of those who seek dragons, their treasure or both—each story weaves a rich tapestry of magic and lore.

Whether it's a battle for survival, the forging of an unlikely alliance, or a humorous twist on hoarding habits, our authors invite you to delve into realms where dragons not only hoard gold but also secrets, spells, and sometimes, even friendships. After all, in the world of dragons, not all treasures are silver and gold—some are stories waiting to be told.

The Hounds of Ardagh – Laura J Underwood

Ginny Ni Cooley never desired more than the simple life she had, living in Tamhasg Wood and using her magic to occasionally assist the folk of Conorscroft while putting up with the machinations of the ghost of her former mentor Manus MacGreeley. But her peace is shattered one night with the arrival of a lad who is fleeing a pack of red-gold hounds led by a hound-shaped demon known as Nidubh.

So much for peace and solitude. By rescuing Fafne MacArdagh, Ginny becomes wrapped in the fabric of an intrigue involving a family feud, a traitorous son, and a blood mage named Edain who is determined to keep her soul. It is she who cast a spell on Fafne's family and household and transformed the MacArdaghs into hounds.

Ginny gives Fafne her word to take him to Caer Keltora so they can report the matter to the Council of Mageborn. But Edain is determined to keep her secret and her soul intact and moves to thwart Ginny at every turn.

For Ginny Ni Cooley who has faced many bogies, dealing with a demon, a bloodmage and the Dark Lord of Annwn will be no easy task. But she will do what she must to undo Edain's spells. If not, Manus' soul will become part of Arawn's Cauldron of Doom. Ginny will become a demon's feast, and poor Fafne will join the Hounds of Ardagh.

Wee Folk and Wise: A Fairies Anthology
– edited by Deby Fredericks

All over the world, fairy tales are told.
There are big fairies and little fairies.
Ugly fairies and pretty fairies.
Wise fairies and silly fairies.
Sweet fairies and scary fairies.

Seventeen authors share their own fantastic fairy tales in this magical collection. What kind of fairy will you meet here?

Infinity – Ted Pennella

In the distant future, when peace between humanity and the artificial intelligences their ancestors created has been settled, Conrad Conner tries to live a quiet and unassuming life in orbit about Jupiter on the city-station Socrates' Odyssey. When Conner's attempt to create a prototypical communication artificial for use by the Sol-Humana Confederation's Stellar Fleet gets derailed by the attempted murder of the very artificial he's created, his life spirals into a mad flight back to Earth to try and save at least his sister's children, if not his sister herself. Past failures and heartaches resurface as seemingly unconnected dots become a plot by the First Admiral to steal not just power over the Confederation, but a secret Conner holds within himself.

A secret not even Conner knows about.

Flatlanders - Mike Sherer

Young theoretical physicist Mickey Haiku has fallen into Eden's trap. She is a much smarter scientist who is intent on saving her own dimension by destroying his. Unbeknownst to either, beings from several yet higher dimensions have their own strategies. This sends the mixed-up pawns off on a wild odyssey through a dozen weird, twisted dimensions. As if this hyper-dimensional odyssey isn't challenging enough for Mickey, he has the additional difficulty of embarking on this whacko tour as a (pregnant!) female. Which means Eden is stuck in Mickey's body. The two are soon forced to cooperate since each holds the other's body hostage.

The strangest relationship this side of the 11th dimension develops between the two.

And more – check out our books at

www.wolfsingerpubs.com

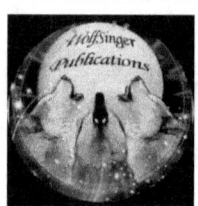